I0594732

Ankh...Ancient Symbol of Eternal Life

SOUL

Artist, Friend and Creator, Mike Garcia

On My Journey…

Shoshana Love is a Visionary, Creative Soul who is here exploring life and sharing with others. She has an MAAT degree in Art Therapy from The School of the Art Institute, Chicago and was founder and director of the The Center for Creative Psychotherapy, Chicago 1985-1994.

Shoshana has led workshops and groups in Chicago, Hawaii, Ashland, Oregon and Santa Fe, New Mexico and has connected with tribal and indigenous people wherever she goes. She sees life as an adventure, and creative expression as our birthright. Shoshana invites you to express what she calls 'The Language of the Soul.'

Nile, Full Moon

Dedication

This book is dedicated to the Creative Soul in ALL of us…and to all those who journeyed with me in and out of form "Heart to Heart." Eternal gratitude!

In memoriam to my Soul Sisters: Sally, Shoshana Rose and Angela.

Also, my Galactic Star Team.

And to Elli who supported me through the delivery.

And to all the courageous souls in Chicago in the groups, private sessions and workshops, learning as I did in that sacred time of our lives.

Love and gratitude to all.

**Sally & I
in Hawaii**

**The Two Shoshanas
in Ashland**

Introduction

Dear Readers,

Welcome to the Sacred Journey of exploring Your Creative Soul!

Thank you being open and having a look at what's inside...not only my book, but what's inside You. Don't let the word 'Creative' throw you off. You don't have to have a Master's Degree in Art History or be able to draw a realistic likeness to be a 'Creative.' We have cell phones for realism, and knowing art history is not related to what I refer to as Our Creative Soul.

The source of creation/creativity, well, I can only say, "It's a God-Job." And the imprint is a code that we all have within.

As a student of Art Therapy, I was walking through the Art Institute one day when I saw a painting that stopped me in my tracks. This painting changed my life; it looked like a child did it. It had a bed flying in the sky (not like Chagall), like a kid would make. I gasped and stood in shock and awe. All I could say to mySelf was, "You can do that? And it's hanging in the permanent collection at the world famous Art Institute of Chicago?"

Freedom! I get to be me.

Isn't that what we all want, to be original to ourselves, in our own way, and in our own style?

My invitation to all of us is to flip the switch from what we call 'art' to Creative Expression, which is a reflection of our Soul.

A single line done by someone who's been afraid to express herself can open doorways. Content is only a part of it. I went to art school 'way back when' and learned to paint realism, but there was no penetration at the heart and soul level. It felt like a hand/eye coordination kind of thing.

The process of creating is a Sacred Journey...one we don't have to 'pack & fly' for.

A word about Soul...dare I talk about it or is it only for the great philosophers of all time? Well, I am talking about Soul. And I've written two books (not published) that explained my version and relationship to this most powerful word. It first appeared in my book Love, Intimacy and the Creative Soul. I went further in my book The Hidden Migration: Uncovering the Journey of the Soul, where I identified the Soul in 5 realms: Physical Soul, Emotional Soul, Spiritual Soul, Galactic Soul, and Creative Soul.

Making our mark is connected to the language of the Soul...ancient, tribal, timeless. It's about the quality of your emotion that gets stirred in you, not the quality of the picture. Trust what is unseen, invisible, cooking, forming. The process can have many twists and turns. Sometimes, a beginning can turn into a warm up, other times it reveals what's to come.

Yes, if you're thinking goes in the direction of perfectionism, judgement, second-guessing, hesitating, not trusting, minimizing and overriding your instinctual Way, you're not alone. We live in a world of images and are bombarded with ways to make things picture-ready.

What's important here is opening to Flow and trusting what wants to be revealed. That's where the Soul inhabits our Creative Expression. That's where the Gold lives.

Welcome to a Journey and a Relationship to yourSelf at the Soul level which includes your child self, your tribal self, ancient self, galactic self as well as your multi-dimensional self, all under what I call Our Creative Soul. This relationship opens the doorways to the inner self… sacred, timeless, unique and original.

Like our dreams, that come from places unknown, so do our images appear when we surrender to what wants to be seen and revealed. They are a mirror, a voice from the Soul level with message and images that are out of time and space. The journey is customized for each of us, and will lead you into a deeper and more intimate connection with yourSelf.

Simple materials can bring enormous rewards…uncovering something that has been hidden from deep inside to honoring it with front row seats.

Our culture values capturing the moment with our cellphones. This is an outer expression of a moment in time. What comes forward when we draw or paint our feelings from within is personal, intimate, original, and reveals the truth of our Emotional Soul, and often feelings we didn't know we had.

The awkward moment that comes when facing the unknown, a blank page, is a small price to pay for the gold that will reveal itself.

Our ancestors, who needed to 'make their mark' with their handprints, brought something forth in a language the soul understands. And to me there's nothing more valuable than knowing who I am at the Soul level.

Let me invite you (a word you'll see throughout the book) to explore, play, feel the YOU that is waiting to appear, Your Version, in Your Way. As for the process, I wrote my book by hand on well over 50 legal pads.

At one point, I did a painting of a fetus born into the night sky, with its umbilical cord trailing off the paper. My unconscious knew something I didn't until the image came out on paper.

Looking for the Source of Creation

BEGINNINGS and ENDINGS...

How we walk into a room, how we end a relationship. Birth and Death, the bigger dimensions of these archetypal themes, we have all navigated and will navigate in our lives.

I began my creative Journey at art school and I learned how to paint realism, a bit, however it was a hand/eye kind of exercise for me. The focus was on the work of art.

When I studied to become an Art Therapist, the focus shifted into my inner Self, which opened me to what I now call My Creative Soul.

I've been blessed to invite fellow Journeyers, like you, to walk the Path with.

Who I was when I began this Journey is not who I am now. I started out imagining I was going to write a memoir with a few 'exercises' at the end. Something happened to me early on in my process, and I felt your Presence. I felt I was being received at the level I was sending (pitcher-catcher.) And it felt so good to me, feeling you Journeying with me, that I continued to tell you stories with Invitations. The book wrote itself, as if I was in conversation with you. I call this Flow, dream come true, fun, and a blessing in my life, as well as a Joyous Healing in my heart. You were with me as a presence every step of the way.

We still do not know the Source of Creation. Yes, the Big Bang theory, but does that really explain why our ancestors were called to create Art/Images and Language? The Source of Creation is in US. It's not just about content or we could "talk" our images.

When we pick up a pen or a chalk or a paintbrush, the physical movement of energy as well as the content, runs through the body, especially the heart chakra. This process creates a connection that is not routed through the mind, it's routed through the emotional body and what I'm calling the Creative Soul.

It's the meeting place of the heart and soul out of time and space. Sacred. It's so original to our Soul - it's the Original Imprint. I call it a "God-Job."

The Ancients left us their images and language. They left us the imprint and Invitation to create our version of the multidimensional Soul. We are Sacred Vessels of Creation, Unique and Original out of time and space.

Many would do a Life Review by looking at photos. For me, going through my writings, my sketchbooks, hundreds of pictures revealed to me my inner Journey. This was the evolution of my Soul, not the different hair dos that I wore. This was Soul Work.

The Baobab has been my favorite tree since I first laid eyes on one in a picture in a book. It is the oldest tree on the planet and this image is a famous image of the Lane of the Baobabs in Madagascar, on an island off the East coast of Africa. This one experience I have not explored in real time. (So far.) It's ancient roots touch me at a Soul level.

Our lives have Archetypal themes, some are emotional, some originate from our individual lineages and some are a spark of divinity that speaks to us in words and images that, when we pay attention, reveal the unique gifts of our Soul's Journey.

Soul Time

"What is time, numbers on a clock?" said my twelve year old Self. I had a hard time understanding how all of civilization routed life through a clock tower (Big Ben in England.) Our culture thinks we've captured time and put it on our wrists.

Time has different flavors. It can be relative, and it can feel timeless. Some people have a different relationship to time, from the inside-out, others from the outside-in. And others can even feel the eternal nature of time.

We Creatives have a different relationship to time. I call it SOUL TIME. That's when our creative juices kick in and we aren't routing through the measurable world, and we are out of relative time and space.

Soul Time invites a perspective of a higher reach and a deeper dive, out of the measurable world and into a range from Ancient to Galactic. This is where our Creative Soul meets life in its many dimensions.

One mark on a paper can open doorways. A 'mistake' in your creative process can lead to a new perspective. In surrendering to Flow, we move out of managing life and into what wants to be revealed, which takes courage.

Invitation: Take a moment and let Soul Time take over. Imagine what wants to be expressed, a feeling, an image, a playing with materials, a piece of writing. It's forming. Journey with your breath, allowing Flow to be your guide.

On the floor, painting before my group The Creative Hour began.

Invitation: Acknowledge yourself for being a Creative

Socrates gave us "Know Thyself..." and in our time, we have experienced multiple ways to know ourselves. Then, we come to "Being Known," letting ourselves be known, and then to being "Knowable."

In my writing to YOU, I'm wanting to set an example, an invitation, to your version of those experiences in the ways I have come to learn them through creative expression, which leads to emotional healing, and fun, and intimacy and and and…

Much as a body-builder would demonstrate and reveal their explorations/ways, or a chef would show their techniques, etc. I am allowing my Self to be knowable to you, the receiver. It is my Path, as they say. I try not to let my ego get in the way.

We are Light Workers, those of you who read this, and it has been my way to bring light into hidden, unloved, uncared-for dimensions of our Soul, in creative ways. Thank you for Journeying with me. Many Mahalos! (as we say in Hawaii)

The Ancients created symbols on cave walls (Art) and language (their stories). We are imprinted with what I call the "Language of the Soul."

The desire and need to create is an imprint in our Soul. We see this in the Ancients across the planet who created words (language) and images (art) and handprints that marked their presence here. Your Creative Soul doesn't lie. It contains themes, issues, emotional truths, and images that appear spontaneously when we face the blank page and surrender to a deeper experience of ourselves.

The paintbrush is in your hands… Heart to heart, with Love, Shoshana

Life Itself is a Work of Art

We are creating all the time. Not all works of art are to last forever. Some are a mere sketch. There are themes. Meeting places are important to me...where I meet another, where I meet myself, where I meet life.

Living a creative life is not defined as something on a canvas done with paint. It is a dimension of living, our very relationship to life itself. It's a mystery, it's magic. It's imagination, it's wonder. It's exploration, it's interest. My Path as a Creative tells a story of a life lived with Color, with Passion, with Wonder and with a desire to experience and explore that vague and abstract word we call Soul. We each have our own Original and Unique version, as unique as our fingerprint. You are the Ultimate Work of Art, the creation so original, a universe is literally inside you.

The Gifts of Journeying as a Creative include:

- Intimacy with yourself
- Getting to know your emotional truths
- Compassion
- Play
- Healing
- A Sense of Self reflected back to you
- Discovery
- Feeling like you're part of Creation

We are The Creatives!

Express Your Version! So have fun...play, wonder, try things out. The process, like life itself, is the Invitation. Blessings on Your Journey. You have been an intimate part of mine. Eternal Gratitude.
  Shoshana

Images: There I am, my 8 year old self, contemplating life, and looking up. It still fits the present day me.

**In the pages of this book, and in our lives, there is a
language that will be revealed in the
invitations offered.**

My invitation is to explore yourself at a Soul Level.

Our Creative Soul includes:

Our Emotional Soul …

Our Physical Soul …

Our Spiritual Soul …

Our Galactic Soul …

As you journey, oftentimes hidden in what appears as
content, is your Soul emerging through the Creative Process.

Honoring it enhances a Sacred Relationship unfolding.

Contents

My First Invitation

This key opens the Sacred Doorway to

Your Creative Soul

The Key is in Your Hands

16

Art Therapy - The Process

There's a stage between painting realism and facing the blank canvas.

Before I was ready to paint without an image, I set up a plant with a coral flower in front of my easel. And wouldn't ya guess, out came a naked woman in water with vines. Picasso invited beautiful models to sit for him, and on his canvas out came cubism, an eyeball over here, a leg over there.

Realism didn't do it for me. If it was only about content, we could just talk our images.

Technology cannot offer us the experience of running it through our hearts and body. When the first laptops came out, I bought a cute, small white one and took it into my tipi and placed it between my legs while I sat directly on Mother Earth, hoping to run creative energy through my 2nd Chakra. No bueno. X marks the spot and that wasn't the spot.

There's a transformation that happens in Art Therapy when your hand touches a material, whether directly or through a paintbrush or pen and the energy and the emotion runs though the arm, routes through the heart and is expressed in form or abstraction that changes the person who is creating it.

Art Therapy offers us the Sacred Invitation to blend our Emotional and Creative Souls. It's a God-Job.

The imprint is already in us. Our Creative Soul emerges and reveals itself in a process through the fingers and the arm, through the heart, when we trust and let go. The pictures are already inside us, waiting for the invitation to be expressed. Trust that the image has its own message to deliver. It's a relationship that calls us to trust the Flow.

This process offers us the wisdom to know ourselves at a Soul Level.

It's not about technique, it's not about painting a nice picture, it's the marriage of the Emotional Soul and Creative Soul.

The Creative Hour
(Back Story)

It's the late 90's and I'm living on Maui.
Photo is Makua, beloved spiritual teacher/Kahuna and me.
A sacred blessing in my life to have met him and experience 4 sacred initiation sessions on the Big Island with him. Eternal gratitude..........

I awoke one morning and felt the need to live in "workshop space." I took all the furniture out of the living room and deemed my space 'The Creative Hour.' One hour a day would be an invitation for me to be creative, in any way and in any form. Also, the hour was just a way we have created sessions of all kinds.

I didn't hold to time (numbers on a clock). And my invitation to You is not about clock time. Some of the most powerful thoughts, feelings, experiences are just moments in eternal time. I painted and felt the flow of Mother ocean supporting me. Living in a sarong added to the feeling of FLOW, which came through in the images. I was not routing through time and space. Fast forward to moving to Ashland, Oregon. First thing I did was rent a gymnasium/studio with an amazing sound system and created a Creative Hour for men and women on Saturday mornings. It was fun and fabulous and wild. Movement, art, feelings, intimacy, fun. Now, I want to invite YOU to join me in the latest incarnation of The Creative Hour.

An invitation is a most powerful offering on many levels.

Each post will be an invitation to write, or draw, and feel, or dance, explore, be....YOU, the extraordinary soul You are.
It's that deep, powerful, original part of who we are.

Custom, unique, a signature, a style, a frequency...It's our unique and original imprint.
Join me whenever You feel called. I'm in the circle with You.
Heart to heart...Shoshana,

Makua and me

The Voice of the Piece

The Voice of the Piece is not a descriptive voice. It is not a voice identifying or reporting in words what is seen in your picture. It's a voice that carries the Heart and Soul of your picture and it's not routed through the mind. Often, this voice has not been heard before, has been hidden, overridden, not received and often not known.

It carries feelings that are tender and unspoken…Sacred Emotional Truths.

Things and feelings are right where we left them, out of time and space. In this Journey we are taking, our hearts are leading the Journey now. As you begin to express your real Self, your Soul Self, your voice from an earlier time in your life, a whole new relationship to our Emotional Soul comes forward to be known and cared for.

Many of the pictures in this book look like a child did them. And she did. The child was closer to her true emotions, unedited, and not routing every feeling through the rational mind first. She has more connection to her feelings, to being spontaneous, less critical, and in wonderment of what would come out. The critical and judgmental voices were overridden by a deeper, more intimate Emotional Truth.

As I began to draw, what came out was often a real surprise to me, and I let it happen. I didn't override it, looking to make a better picture. I learned to trust whatever image wanted to be revealed at the time. If we can be with our image without judgement and criticism, we can learn something about ourselves and open to a hidden part of our Soul.

For me, it has helped me to live more from the inside-out, rather than the outside-in.

Womb Room

This image appeared and when I looked at it, I knew my Soul was looking for an outlet. Years later, I looked at the image and thought, "I'm looking for connection." Sometimes, our interpretations can change over time.

There is a personal initiation...

Every day say out loud, "I Am A Creative!"

And, put on your favorite song and move the body in ways that support your opening.
And, invite your friends and beloveds if you feel called.

We're getting ready.

also, have a little sit down chat with your inner child, inner critic, any part of you that may
interrupt the new pattern that is wanting to be expressed....comfort them, invite them along,
and then take some restoring breaths and get ready to journey.

The Family of my Heart, 1982

It surprised me to have an image reveal itself without routing it through the mind, and although I didn't have the word 'Soul' then, it appeared anyway.

This image appeared as the feeling I wanted to have with my family.

Invitation: First Drawing

I want to begin with acknowledging each of You, spiritual, creative beings, for the paths You
have walked and are walking, for your openness to explore and learn more about your
multidimensional, creative Selves.

In the face of all the destruction we see in the world, we are called to meet it with creation.

I am truly blessed to contribute what I can.

Let's Begin….

Warm Up:
Preparing the canvas (which is You).
One minute of conscious deep breathing feeling the inner You. We're unplugging from the outer
and from the mind....moving into inner journeying space.

Remember:
YOU, we, are the Ultimate Work of Art. We're getting out of the mind and inviting in free space.
We're finding and connecting with parts of ourselves we may have needed to leave behind.
NO MÁS!

Grab a pen, pencil, whatever.
Back of an envelope, a blank piece of paper, something to draw on.
Look around the room or wherever you are and draw where your eyes land. Don't shoot for
realism. We've got our cell phones for that. Just let it out...CUSTOMIZE! (One of my all-time
favorite words)

Voice of the Piece:

Don't describe what you've drawn.
Give it a voice.
Let it speak from it, AS it.
Write down those words.

Sit back and listen to those sacred words.
You opened a doorway.
Breathe and digest those words and feelings.

Heart to Heart…

Invitation: Field Trip to an Art Store

optional: if it's not in the budget...a pencil and paper.
           Picasso created his famous picture of a woman
           in 3 lines

Loose paper or a spiral journal
A watercolor pad of paper (140 lbs works well)
-customize the size to meet what feels right for you
Box of Artist's Soft Pastels
A couple of black sharpies, fine point (not extra fine point)
A tray/set of watercolors (no tubes that take time to open)
and/or Watercolor Crayons (CARAN D'ACHE)
Two or three different sized paint brushes
A couple of your favorite pens
A small glue gun with glue sticks
Canvas bag for when we go on art walks
Notepad for ideas
A bar of green LAVA soap for cleaning up hands and brushes (hardware store)

Heart to heart

My Indoor Studio

Invitation: Moving the Whole Self Forward
(a writing exercise)

For those who have felt even a tinge of abandonment, this invitation is for Us.

We are inviting the child within onto the Creative Journey. She/he is included, wanted, valued, cared for and has a seat on their throne as well. In fact, at times the paintbrush is in her/his hands.

We are writing a letter to our inner child, telling them how much they are seen and knowable. Memories and feelings may come flooding in. Journey with him/her remembering moments and experiences they navigated alone. Tell them they have support, space, and your invitation...a most powerful and loving gift.

Let Your heart feel them and write their words, then speak them aloud in a way that wasn't possible back then.

Notice how this validates and comforts them. It is the gift they always wanted.

Siri, my Sacred Bear named after Sirius, brightest star in the sky with the naked eye.

Invitation: "Spring is in the Air"

Aloha and good morning Creatives! Spring is in the air. Take a moment and breathe it in. Making space for something creates our next invitation. How we fill it, live in it, what our relationship to it is, speaks volumes, and space is not square footage. We're looking for creative space, imagination space, inner space, free space.

Our warm up is creating space with our breath on the inner. With your feelings of spring in the air make a picture, your version, of Spring. Think earthing/birthing, opening, wondering. We're "blooming"!

Spring in Santa Fe

Invitation: Art from the Heart

On a large piece of your paper, draw a heart. Write feelings that appear, the messages that your heart wants to share with you. Pay attention to your breathing. Are there secret hiding places? Are there spots that have a "do not disturb" sign on them? Let your heart talk to you. It's personal - real personal. You can write on your picture if you like and the invitation is to feel what's Your's to feel. Things and feelings are right where we left them. The voice of your heart is comforted by your loving attention.

Heart to Heart

Invitation: Free Space

Let something come through you. Begin without knowing where you're going or what's coming through. Override the mind. There's an entire genre of art called "Abstract Expressionism" - Do your version.

"Creativity is the doorway to your Emotional Soul"
 Shoshana Love

Jackson Polluck - Abstract Expressionism
Image Source: https://www.bohaglass.co.uk/jackson-pollock-art/

Invitation: Your Unique Style... CUSTOMIZE!

"The style of the person is the style of the person."
<u>Shoshana Love</u>

There is a difference between reporting and sharing. One can be sourced from the mind while the other can come from feelings of the heart.

In our relationship to one's Self and to Other (as if there is other) emotional connection is key. It carries the very depth of Being of heart & soul.

I call it the Language of the Soul. It also carries sound (more about that in the coming times).

I grew up with what I call "packaging"... living from the outside in.

My offering originates from the inner, living from the inside out, creating from the inside out... being original to one's Self.

Creativity is a doorway to many things. For me, I'll call it, Healing with Art, a Spiritual Journey.

Even when working from the outside, we still want to leave space for our own Unique Style to emerge.

Hide on the Wall

Invitation: Hands

Draw a picture of your hands. They are sacred. Picasso's mother put his drawings on the fridge. After you make your version(s) of your hands, display your picture.

Value your Originality!

My hands in ceremony with Maasai women

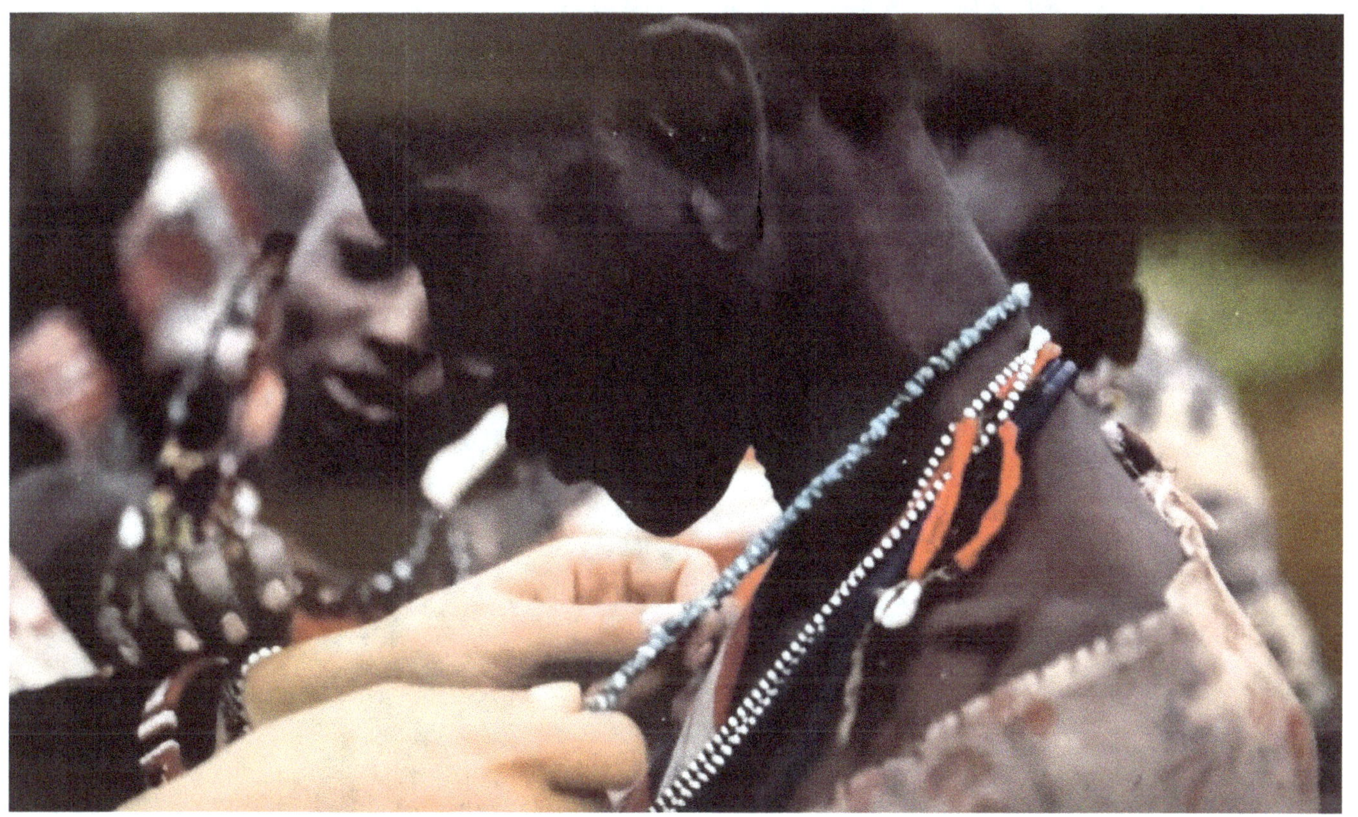

Invitation: Going Public: Sketching Outdoors

The weather is changing, it's time to Go Public!

It might feel a little different at first to go to a park and take out your sketchbook. It's fun, and you are in the company of many of our great masters.

Find a place that you're called to, look around 360 degrees until you're inspired by something, and customize, in your own style.

Remember, we have our cell phones for realism. We are creating the reality of our own worlds, and see if some creative writing wants to accompany your drawing/watercolor.

P.S. I brought a portable easel to Santorini and painted those famous blue and white silhouettes. It was fabulous fun for me.

Back in Chicago, at Lincoln Park Zoo, I brought my sketchbook to the Big Cat House. Hearing the bellowing sounds of the lions roar vibrating against those walls and cages was unforgettable. And kids gathered around and were inspired by my art...which of course, looked like a child did them. Made me happy, and made a great memory!

We inspire others!

FORM: Being in the right Form for you

Some people paint pictures of pots, others make them in 3D.

Being in the right Form is key. This form...I call Pitcher-Catcher...being received at the level and at the moment in real time, is custom for me.

You, my Creative Hour Journeyers, are THE PERFECT FORM for me. Fast, wild, creative, alive in real time, in the moment, is my style.

"The style of the person is the style of the person...straight across the board"
 <u>Shoshana Love</u>

You are fundamental in what is happening to me, from me, through me, as me, right now.
I feel received, known, heard, considered, and connected. I've always said "I just need the right imprint." You are that major imprint for me. I have written 8 books and 2 children's books, none published. It's not that I couldn't have found my way to publish, it's that the FORM (among other things like support) was not right for me.

Have a look at your style and what FORMS suit your expression, support you, celebrate you.

As Socrates offered us his extraordinary and simple wisdom, "Know Thyself" and I add, "at a Soul Level."

Invitation: War and Our Inner Battles

Our art is a safe space for our feelings. What can we do when we are stirred to our core with upset in our outer world.

Creativity gives us an outlet for our feelings, a safe space to meet parts of ourselves that are also difficult to manage and digest.

Take one of your papers and materials, find your center and let out and give expression to how you feel impacted by these painful and cruel energies.

Pablo Picasso, Guernica, 1937

EQUALIZER MARKET
by Singer
JK

pizza

Reaching Beyond (Create your own Version)

Explore outside your habitat and see what and who crosses your Path.

At the equator I had my sketchbook with me. Sitting down on Mother Earth, with my art bag and sketchbook, I took out my watercolors and began to paint. A man approached and I reached my arm out for connection. He met me with his. Then, his friends joined in and surrounded us. I tore out pages from my sketchbook and invited them to paint with me. These are their pages, which they gave to me and I share with you here. I treasure them, the moment, and their creative expressions.

We all had fun and created an experience together that was unforgettable.

African Brothers' Artwork at the Equator

Invitation: The Paintbrush is in your Hands

When I first came to Santa Fe decades ago, I was called to go to the art store, then on Canyon Road, Artisan. Inside, carefully displayed on one wall were rows and rows of paintbrushes. I took a picture of it, because it was beautiful, and I had never seen anything like that. I imagined all the art that would/could come from that display. Then, I spotted the biggest brush I had ever seen (in the photograph here). Of course, I bought it, not knowing if I'd ever use it. It's size was immense to me. So I took it home, back to Chicago, and put it on my desk and looked at it as if it were a piece of sculpture.

Fast/forward years later, I used it when I could match the energy of such large strokes.
No matter the size, each brush carries an invitation.

Be with one of your brushes. When it calls to you, answer the call. That is the invitation for today.

Edvard Munch, "The Scream"

Invitation: Archetypal Images

Archetypal Images are themes, symbols, ancient patterns, stories, roles, identities, images, etc…

Back in the 80s, in my women's groups in Chicago, what came out of them, through them, was amazing for me to witness. These images were often simple and yet their emotional truths were what I will call Archetypal Images.

One such image repeated was Edvard Munch's "The Scream."
Another, was Georgia O'Keeffe's version of Flowers (see image below). These clients had not seen and did not know either of these artists and had not seen their artwork.

We have themes and feelings and images deep in our SOUL. I call them "Sacred Images," Archetypal Images. They are some of the extraordinary gifts of our Creative Soul and I'll add Emotional Soul as well.

In my last book, My Archetypal Life, I saw how certain themes were Ancient, in the collective, and part of my Soul's journey as well.

Sit quietly and consider some of your Archetypal Themes. For example: loneliness, fear, longing, freedom, isolation, love, anger, bonding, angelic, cruelty, joy.

When you feel ready, choose one of the above or any theme that arises, and express your version of an Archetypal Image.

You/We are not alone. Blessings on your Sacred Journey!

Georgia O'Keeffe "Red Canna" 1924

Invitation: Walking a Labyrinth- Your Sacred Journey

It's a new season. If there isn't a labyrinth in your town, create your own unique sacred journey, step by step in a neighborhood park etc.

As we know, the labyrinth is a sacred symbol. It mirrors the Milky Way Galaxy we inhabit and are sourced from. (I know, it's a God Job.)

Walking a labyrinth can be a sacred act, an invitation to journey with our relationship to the cosmos, as well as a life review and a promise for tomorrow.

Invite your own CUSTOM version of the path.

"Each step in love" was the directive given to us, a group of 6 in Ashland, Oregon. (Remember, Ileah?) We walked the labyrinth on a mountain in Ashland, bees from the nearby hives swarming our steps. Magic!

In your right moment, write and draw what the labyrinth revealed to you.

I love to make labyrinths. When I lived in Maui, I'd make them on the beach for people to walk. This is a small version of a labyrinth in my backyard, along with my Galactic Chamber (arch) for viewing the stars.

Horses at Bishop's Lodge, Santa Fe

Mom, Dad & Baby, Too

Invitation: "Getting the Bucks Out"
(As in lunging your horse before taking it on the trail)

The warm-up in our creative process is fundamental to who in us is creating. Feeling tuned-up begins the process of inspiration. Living-tuned up is the frequency I call "aliveness."

How important is a warm up? It's like flipping the switch to "on." It's key to restoring our FLOW. Do a warm up even if you don't express it on paper or with color...we have Creative Minds we want to keep open, too.

Take your sketchbooks and find something interesting to sketch on the outer or do a feeling picture from the inside.

Elli's Warm Up

Invitation: Letting Your Eternal Inner Child Come Out

Einstein gave us "Imagination is more powerful/important than knowledge." I'm not sure what the exact quote is. Whatever he said, I'll claim the other unused word.

Another journey outside with your Inner Child this time. Stop a dog walker, find a budding flower, a tree that calls to you and don't limit yourself to one image/picture. Pick up found objects for add-ons with glue when you get home. Realism is not needed. CUSTOMIZE!

For my three pictures I had fun, I used spit, I sat on the ground and they delight me. Play invites the "frisky" out.

Llamas in Ashland, Oregon

Invitation: The Healing Image - Bow & Arrow

When I worked with others, I often asked them to draw what I call "The Healing Image." For me, I was always "reaching for my father" not in real time, not in the outer world, in my inner self. So, I drew a picture of my arms reaching for him. It felt good to express it in an image on paper.

Years later, the image of Bow & Arrow came strong into my consciousness and into my life. While on retreat with a group in Taos, someone brought a bow & arrow and the target for us to have fun with. I had never seen or used one before. When my turn came, I took a stance, pulled back the bow and let the arrow go. Cachink! It hit the bullseye. Amazing. No wonder that Yoga pose always felt comfortable for me.

Years later, a client, now friend, brought me a gift. It is an ancient bow and arrow with feathers and leather from Africa. Why she brought it, I'll never know. One of those things I call a "God-Job." I use this sacred experience to illustrate that anything can be a Healing Image.

Draw your version of a Healing Image for you. Then sit with it and let it penetrate. It is sacred because you brought it out from the hidden inner self into the light.

The bow and arrow has become an archetypal image for me. Leonardo's version of a triangle in a circle is an archetype representing polarities for me. The further one pulls back into the darkness, allows for greater expansion into the light.

**African Bow and Arrow
from Kasey & Olive**

Ankh Staff with Maasai Beaded Cloth

**Ankh, Symbol for Eternal Life
Mike Garcia, Artist**

Invitation: Dreams Come True

The Ankh is an ancient sacred symbol from Egypt representing the word "life" and is a symbol of life itself.

I have always been drawn to and loved the Ankh. In 1996, I was in Egypt and entered a sacred tomb, saw an Ankh carved on a wall, barely visible in the hands of a queen. I literally stopped breathing and asked my boyfriend to take a picture of my hands meeting the hands of a queen holding an Ankh.

The Ankh has touched me on a soul level and now mainstream culture recognizes it too. Dreaming out loud I mentioned to my friend Mike Garcia, an over the top amazing artist/ creative, "Mike, I've always wanted my own Ankh."

He said, "Draw it." On a big piece of paper, I drew an outline, very primitive and childlike, of an Ankh. He said, "OK." Then, I said, "Could you add a snake up the front, and a star on top?" This is what he brought me, can you believe it? Takes my breath away. It is my most valued sacred possession. I use it/hold it, and speak into the oval my wishes and messages for gratitude.

My Hands Touching the Ancient Wall

Invitation: Make Your Mark

Feeling connected to our true and authentic and real self is a Journey. It's not always about the content of what emerges, it's about the process, about finding parts of Self that may be hidden and scared to reveal.

Years ago, I worked with a client who said she couldn't draw. I invited her to choose a color that she was drawn to. She chose red. Then she waited, breathed, contracted, and in a bold moment she made a big red mark on the page. In that moment, that gesture opened doorways that had been closed and locked for decades, perhaps generations and sobbing came out from deep inside her.

In your right moment, choose a color, breathe, and with big energy in your body, make your mark. Then feel what's yours to feel and when you're ready, write about it.

After all, Freud came up with ink blotches to diagnose psychological states.

There's a Universe in this gesture…both in energy and in feeling.

Living in Hawaii

My art revealed my inner journey that I wasn't aware of until it showed up in these pictures.

Invitation: The Elements

Years ago, I was thinking about what is the most powerful element. At that time, I decided it was the wind.

In Santorini, I was there during a wind storm. Shopkeepers pulled their gates down in front of their shops and everyone ran to take cover. I felt in my body chased by the wind. And I wrote a piece about the wind being the most powerful element. It moves the ocean, and it stirs the blood in our bodies.

We are all of the elements, including others that are not measurable. Choose one: wind, fire, water, earth and draw your version of your relationship/feelings about this element.

Under Water Feeling Scared

A Powerful Journey

Some experiences are so powerful there are no words to express them. Taking to my watercolors gave me the outlet to attempt to record and reveal something I had no words for. And like we treasure souvenirs from important experiences and events in our lives, this picture is a reminder of something that appeared that was beyond language for me.

Eyes in the Vines

During a sacred Ayahuasca journey eyes appeared in the plants and I captured them in this drawing.

Images of the Same Feeling

Sometimes we are not finished
exploring with one drawing. We need
to make more.
(As in Monet's Water Lillies)

Invitation: Touch Is Sacred

I grew up in an emotionally and physically distant family, so of course the Journey to know myself was definitely highlighted. Physical touch was absent.

So I began looking for examples of people touching as a way of connecting. Back in the '90s, Bill Clinton stood out to me in the way that he could comfortably wrap his arm around a boy or another person that he didn't know. Mother Teresa was another example for me: her capacity to reach out to people who were severely physically compromised and kiss their pain.

I'm crying as I write this...for humanity.

In these times where we use technology so often to connect, touching another can be a gift at the Heart and Soul level. It may feel awkward at first to even touch a friend's arm, but the human connection at the physical level touches way more than a piece of skin.

Elli, my assistant/gift from God is crying as she types this. And we are touching.

Invitation: Write a Chapter of Your Life

We are all authors. You are the authority of your life. We have stories and chapters of our Journey.

In your right moment, let a sacred moment come into your consciousness and Journey with that on the inner. When you are ready, take out a favorite pen and write what that moment meant to you, where it touched you on the inner and why it comes to your consciousness in this moment.

Remember when I shared "The Paintbrush is in Your Hands?" Now we're adding "The Pen is in Your Hands, too."

Food: A Chapter of My Life

Honoring a theme in a Sacred Way

Handmade Book on My Relationship to Food

Invitation: Have a go at it! Write Your Poem

I was never into poetry, not that I read it and didn't like it. I just wasn't drawn to it.

One day, I was sitting in my doctor's waiting room, (a multi-dimensional healer) looking at all the books he had stacked up. Most were poetry books.

One caught my eye. It was called Star Gazing. Whoa, I'm a star person. More about that later. (I wrote a book called Reaching for the Stars) So I picked up the book and read through it. The author really knew the stars. It wasn't Moon, June, Spoon rhyming. Some of the poems were one paragraph, others were 2 pages long. Then, I looked at the author's name on the front. Miriam Sagan, Carl's niece. Well, I was inspired. So I went home and wrote a dozen poems, my own version. She gave me permission without knowing it, changing my idea of what poetry could be.

Then I wrote my most famous poem on relationships. I will share it with you now. It is only two words:

"...And You?"

Tribal Eyes

Invitation: Eyes... Look in the mirror and draw your eyes. What do you see?

I'd like to share two experiences relating to eyes that penetrated me out of time and space. Many years ago, I was at a dolphin sanctuary in the Keys and each of us were given a dolphin to escort us to the other side of the inlet. I was given the largest dolphin, named Sherri. At that time, my name was Sherri as well. I grabbed onto her fin and she turned and looked at me. Our eyes met and I had the feeling of looking into 25 million years ago.

The second experience I was in the desert of Israel, where you see beige 360 degrees. My group was in a Land Rover. There were six of us. What seemed out of nowhere a Bedouin appeared carrying a staff with six sheep following along. This was so dream-like. Our Rover stopped and he walked up to my window and we looked into each other's eyes. I felt like I was looking into 5,000 years ago.

These two experiences changed me fundamentally. They are sacred and eternal moments in my Journey. Their eyes told their stories, feelings and Soul Connections…

As do ours.

Images: Eyes have appeared in so many of my pictures. It's been said that eyes are the windows of the Soul.

Invitation: Sound...a Profound Language.

Tune in, Tune up, to how sound impacts you

In my early twenties, I was watching a Good Morning America type show and Marlo Thomas and Gloria Steinam were having a conversation. I don't remember the content. What stood out to me was when one spoke the other responded with a sound of empathy and care, no words were spoken at that moment. That connection touched me deeply. That's when I knew that, for me, content and words were less important than sound. Sound that comes from the Heart.

So that kind of flipped the switch for me to look at sound over content. The sound of the crack of a bat, the sound of a back hand tennis return, the sound of mourning, the sound of fear, the sound of joy. We don't need language for these moments. This comes directly from the heart and soul.

Before there were drums, Africans used the body, slapping patterns with their hands on the body to create rhythm and sound.

Before there were flutes, there were birds that made sounds and those sounds were heard and we created rattles and flutes.

Truth has a sound, Pleasure has a sound, we are Creative Vessels and our sounds express our emotional truth.

Some of my Sacred Instruments

Invitation: Making Space for our Pain

Years ago, I discovered the word Pain in Paint and was led to do workshops that I called "Paint Your Way Through the Holidays." The first response to pain might be "Help!" and "Get me out of this!" - There's an old saying, "If you can't get out of it, get into it."

A few months ago, I was sad and in emotional pain. The arrow was pulled back far. I sat down with my chalks and I didn't think about an image or plan it. I didn't go through my mind first. When the image appeared, I didn't know what it was. After many days, I looked at it, and knew. So I wrote on the picture "I'm lying here, looking at a part of myself dying."

Making space for all feelings is about not rejecting any part of myself. There are gifts in the pain. It allows me to know myself deeper. Without the dark we're not going to see the stars. After I did this picture and figured out what it was, I felt free…and in my emotional truth.

Invitation: Create Your Version of a Self Portrait

Our soul carries ancient imprints that come out in creative ways: dreams, art, stories.
Be with your materials, place the mind aside. You can use a mirror or not, and be open to what your creative juices express.

Over the years, I've come to know that anything and everything can be a Self Portrait. Decades ago, when I was a student at the Art Institute in Chicago, I took a course where we were invited to do Self Portraits. I did 12, all while looking in a mirror, and all came out as tribal men and one came out looking like Jesus. Was this past lives? Soul Level?

My First Self Portrait

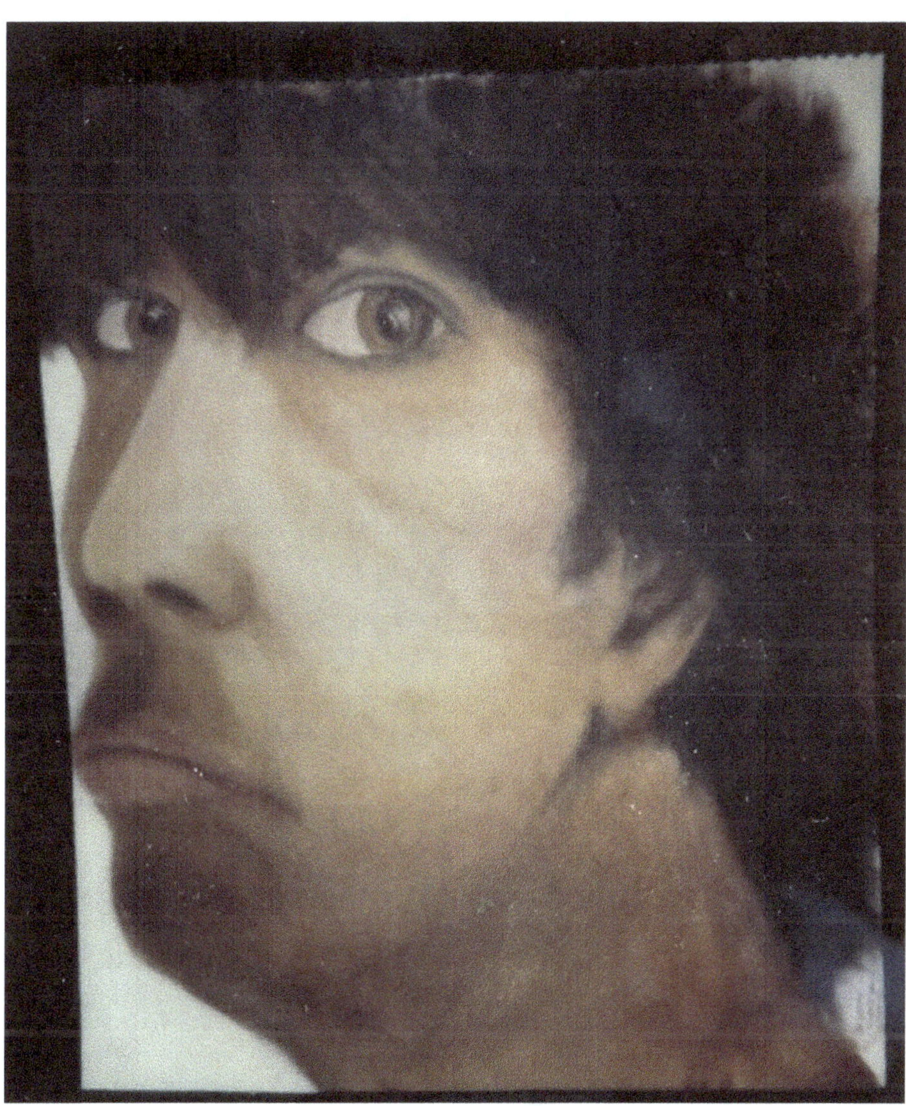

A Picture is Worth 1,000 Words

An invitation into one of my writing tables:

Invitation: Reaching... Speaking Your Healing Image

I had a conversation/healing with a friend last night. We've been through a lot together. Met here in Santa Fe in 1994, she on her motorcycle, me walking down Canyon Road. "Wanna get on back?" she asked. "Yes," I replied, never having been on a 'bike' before.

As we were riding, I felt uneasy. I said, "Can you take me to a motorcycle shop? I'm not a backseat rider." We went. I bought a bike. She gave me a quick lesson in the parking lot and off we went. Weeks later we raced our motorcycles in the Plaza at midnight.

We both have been through a lot together, both of us therapists. Last night I reached out to her. I was in the middle of having a new interpretation about a big chunk of my life. It was a first for me to reach out like that.

She shared with me her version of the same theme. After a good hour or more on the phone, I said to her, "I feel like I was in quicksand and I reached out for help and you gave me your hand and helped pull me out."

Her understanding was a healing for me. I write this to you, because the word 'reaching' has a lot of different images and meanings. My healing image was two hands...mine reaching up to her, hers meeting mine.

What does reaching mean to you at this moment? If you feel called, see your image or draw it, or speak into it.

Invitation: Destiny...Support from the Unseen

My husband did not approve of my first center, its location. It was on Halstead Street in Chicago before it was developed and gentrified. The woman who had the gallery on the first floor "packed a gun" as it was then considered a dangerous neighborhood. I didn't see danger, I saw possibly, hope, a place of my own that I could create in ways that were Custom to me. I thought it was my offering to the community but looking back I can see I was also looking for my own center inside.

He screeched away in his car and left me there. Wild horses wouldn't/couldn't stop me. I signed the lease. It was a sacred moment of possibility in my life. What happened next I could not have imagined. I called my first center, Center for Creative Psychotherapy, and peeled off the letters for the front window. Then I found a neon artist and I drew the words Art Therapy on a piece of paper. Weeks later he presented me with my neon sign which hung outside the front window. I wanted those words to be seen all lit up and known by passerbys lighting up a creative field that was not yet in the collective.

I wanted to create a place that offered something more than sharing the recycled stories of our painful and often isolating childhoods. I wanted to invite creative expression into healing. Walking up that spiral staircase to the second floor where my first center was located, was for me, a commitment like some people feel when walking down the aisle. It was an archetypal walk for me.
It was scary, I was scared, I'd lift each leg up with my arms step by step for days until I could "stand on my own two feet." This was 1985.

Invitation: Distracting and Overriding the Mind…

"Breaking the Code"

Is there something you haven't mastered, wished you could do, haven't been able to do yet? From the first time I saw and heard a didgeridoo being played, I knew I wanted to be in the tribe of people who walked the earth and could play the didge. Not so easy... Getting circular breathing is something, shall we say, otherworldly. How do you keep the breath/sound going when you need to inhale and take a breath?

I wanted it so badly that at the time I said, "If someone gave me the choice 1 million dollars or circular breathing, hands down it was circular."

I tried for years, took lessons, prayed, slept with my didge, no bueno, couldn't get it. My mind always said, "You just ran out of breath. Do I need an extra chromosome to keep this thing going?"

Back story… one day by happenstance I was in a park in the suburbs of Chicago and there was a 1 mile race going on. I had gym shoes on and wanted to be a part of it, so I walked up to the front of the pack and decided to give it a go.

Running with them I was engaged in being with them, looking at the scenery, forgetting that I hadn't done a full mile in my own practice yet. Then, voila! I did it! "How could this be?" I asked myself. Then, after I sat down and cried, I figured it out.

My mind had been occupied, overridden by the spontaneity of the moment. I was totally engaged in the Journey.

Fast forward to living in Ashland, Oregon. It was late one night and I took out my didge to try again. I put on the CD (dating myself here) that my friend Astarius gave me years ago. He was a didge player and he would walk around carrying his didge. I wanted what he was having. I put on the didge CD and began to blow into it, huff puff, take a breath, blow again. Then a miracle happened. I was just listening, no mind, forgot about what I was doing with my huffing and puffing, just putting all my attention on HIS playing. In the blink of an eye, after over a decade of trying, the sound came through, no stopping, a continuous sound. I sat down and sobbed.

That night, I broke the code. My mind was totally distracted, not resisting with thinking that I had to stop and take a breath.

Then I did the next thing my friend/teacher, Sage, from northern Wisconsin, told me, "When you learn something, teach it."

So I began teaching Didge Classes, and had my students play while they focused on my mouth and breath, to use distraction of mind to help. Two students over time got it. Breaking the code, being in "the Flow," meant everything to me. Inside, a part of me felt like an ancient member of "the Tribe" of humans from long ago, connected to that ancient sound.

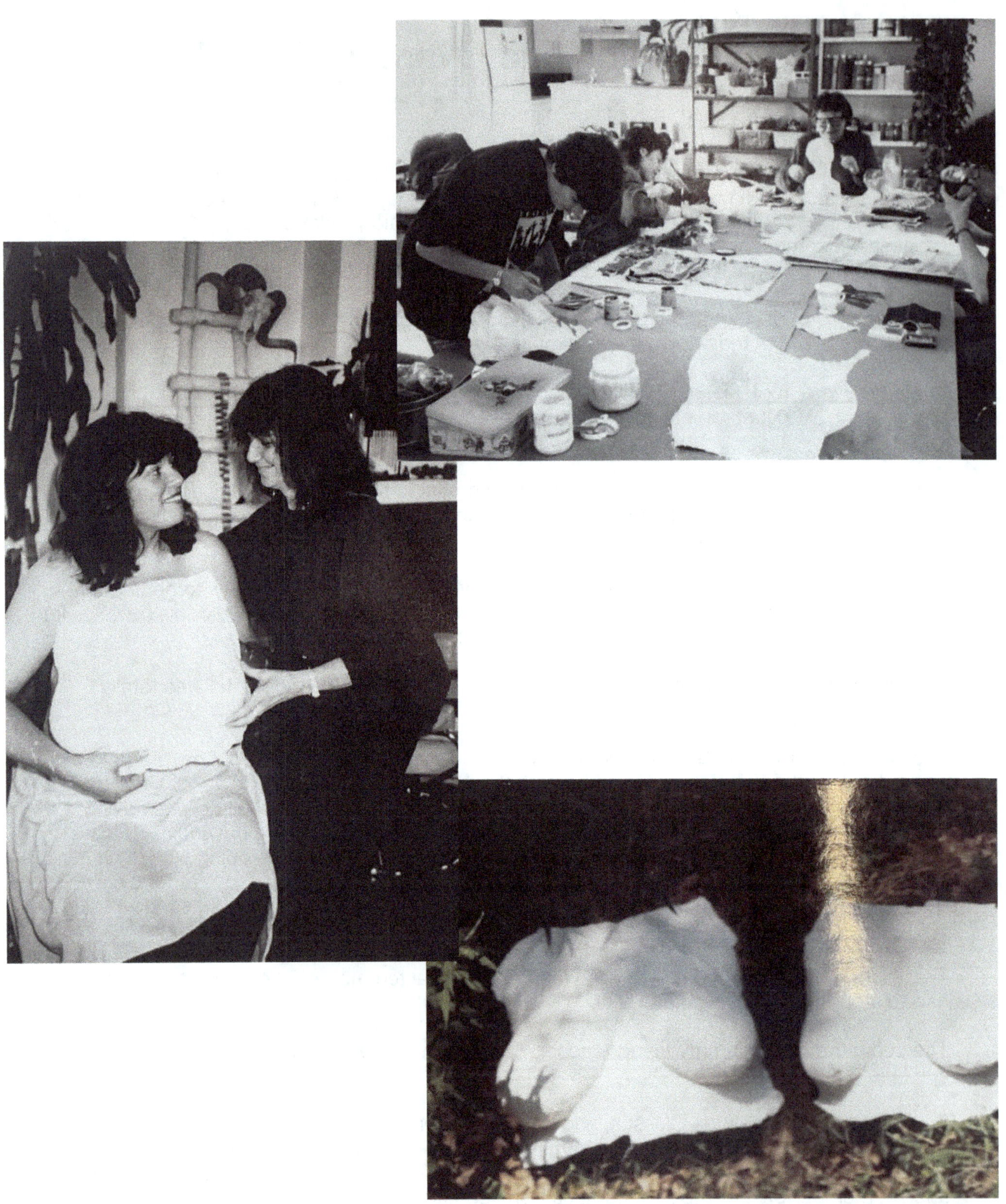

Invitation: Honoring the Feminine

In one of my women's groups, I invited them to experience and explore something experimental. "Do we want to use art to honor our breasts?" All were in. This is back in the '80s in Chicago. BOLD.

We partnered up and used the same materials we used to do masks on our faces for covering our breasts. When the molds dried, embellishments were added. Then we took our sculptures out to the forest and photographed them in the trees.

At the same time, a local gallery was displaying a show on breast cancer, which we attended. Our world is our canvas. Our bodies are a work of art. Our breasts not only nourish life and create pleasure, they are a Sacred Work of Art.

To Keep it Real...

I shared one image of my writing space, and there are two... One is a six-foot round and the other is an eight-foot rectangle table in the center of my living room with two big chairs.

SPACE! My favorite element (more about that later).

A Field Trip to the Lincoln Park Zoo to see the Vulture's Nest.
(I was into nests then, and in this photo we stopped to see the seals.)

Women's Group "Childhood Field Trip"

Back in Chicago, I led/created five women's groups that lasted over five years each. I asked the groups to also meet on their own each week, so as you can imagine, deep relationships were formed and there was lots of support for each other.

Thinking back to this story I'm about to share is an amazing mind-blowing experience... that could only happen because all members were born in Chicago, unlike gatherings today where people gather from very different locations.

I had an idea to create a "field trip" with one group. We would journey to each of our Childhood Homes, to be "witnesses" and to experience and feel who we were back then. Everyone signed up their addresses and one of the women provided the van, another coordinated the addresses and made a route for us to follow.

The day arrived and one by one we journeyed to different neighborhoods and parked in front of each home. Getting out of the van, we circled hand in hand as some women knocked on doors, some told stories and there were lots of tears and memories.

Having the support of the group, with their eyes to witness a piece of childhood memory, their roots, was so deeply intimate, an experience that is so unique, so touching the hearts of both our inner and outer childhoods, it's still unbelievable to me now.

They asked me to write my address down too. When we got out of the van to my apartment, and I stood there looking up, flooded with emotion and shock, what came to my mind was, "How did all those feelings and experiences fit into that small space?"

Invitation: Imagine your version of this experience, and include whoever you would want to be standing with you as witness and support.

Invitation: Customize Your "Vision Quest"

When Native American consciousness came to me back in the Chicago days, I wanted to combine the consciousness of what I wrote my thesis on, Separation Issues, with a Vision Quest. So, I took one of my women's groups on a "Vision Quest" to Harms Woods in the suburbs of Chicago, for a Custom-made experience.

Intention is key. Of course, on so many levels it's a Customized version, but still with the right intention, a powerful experience can be had.

The drumming began and we all separated, explored, walked around, and then sat on blankets we brought, each alone, with our own thoughts and feelings...for three hours. Then the sound of my drum brought us back together in circle. Powerful feelings and visions were shared.

I had a huge bungie cord custom made to 30' with polar fleece fabric sewn around it. I also had a 15' one made. We used them to symbolize an experience of separation. Two by two, the women went inside the womb-made rope and pulled and moved and created an experience of connection and separation, each pair creating their own endings: tugging, dropping the rope, fighting, all experiences 'in the body' of their version of separation. This was powerful. Years of stored-up energy got expressed in their own unique Custom made ways.

P.S. Years later, I used my bungie cords laid on the ground as a womb in my Goddess workshops… "All Petals Open."

"All Petals Open" Workshops

When I left Hawaii and moved back to the mainland, Hawaii didn't leave me. It was not long before I created my 'All Petals Open' workshops for women. Being reborn into the arms, hearts and sacred Womb of the Great Mother.

I'd set up the space, sarongs for all women to change into, and position my two bungie cords into a large Yoni / Womb in the center of the room. One by one, the women approached the Yoni with the support of the drum and entered into the sacred space while the rest of us sat on the floor surrounding her. Each took their turn one by one and claimed her space in the center.

We sat around the Sacred Womb, and I provided beautiful long stemmed roses to be used as paintbrushes, each of us softly, gently, caressing the woman's hair, face, hands, body with the roses. In two of the workshops the women, one by one, dropped their sarongs and stepped into this sacred rebirth experience, naked. They even included me in one of the workshops, insisting I go into the womb experience as well.

We were Re-Born into love, with women, as women.

Then we did Womb-Dancing, and I'd show them some hula moves as we swayed to Hula Music (although I was a beginner when I moved to Hawaii, the first thing I did was take Hula Lessons).

Invitation: Feeling FLOW

It's Spring now, and the waters are running. I discovered this way back in Ashland (Oregon) as I was standing on a bridge in Lithia Park. The waters were running and I was holding onto the metal rail, while standing with my feet somewhat apart.

Then, I felt the flow of the river/creek penetrate my body. The flow of waters was coming from behind and moving forward. What an amazing sensation, a gift from Mother Earth. Then, I crossed over to the other side of the bridge and felt the waters coming toward me 'incoming.' Today, in Santa Fe, the waters were flowing hard and it reminded me of the frequency of FLOW...

Invitation: Hop on over to a Park you know that has such a stream and bridge, and experience your version. It's the Source of Life.

Image: The Acequia Madre (Mother Ditch)
Wars were fought way back when over this flow.

Invitation: Mother Earth...Belly to Belly

African Wood Sculpture

In recent times, we are hearing much about Earthing... walking barefoot on Mother Earth. Now, they have shoes designed for this, where the soles (souls) are less encumbered with artificial materials so that we can feel a closer connection to Her.

I offer another connection, more primary.

For those of us who did not feel the imprint of intimacy with our mothers, I invite you to be on Mother Earth, front of your body lying Belly to Belly (face turned toward the side) and feel the surrender, feel the connection, feel the bond. And let the mind go out of identity and surrender into the deeper connection, prior to identity. And breathe and feel.

When you feel called, let your pen or art materials speak to you.

Costa Rica: Workshop on the Chakras

Back in the '90s I flew to Costa Rica to a workshop on the Chakras. The plane landed at midnight in San Jose, and it was my plan to stop at the International Market at the airport and get my candy bar, Toblerone.
Being a chocolate addict, those airport shops got me through lots of Overseas travel. But, the shop was closed.
I had no time for panic, as the airport was a scene of madness and I had to get a cab to take me to the Retreat Center somewhere in the hills of central Costa Rica.
The next morning, the group of around 30 gathered in a big pavilion, just beautiful, with amazing natural foliage and the sound of birds. Though my attention was on meeting new people from far-away lands, a part of me was fretting on the inside thinking about how and where I was going to get my fix of chocolate.
One by one, we stepped up to the mic to introduce ourselves and share something. My breathing had quickened because part of my attention was on needing chocolate and how the hell was I going to get it?
When my turn came, I had a "come to Jesus" moment. Could I reveal and share what was going on inside me and risk making a real bad first impression?
I shook as I took my turn at the mic, and though I didn't plan it, out came "Hello everyone, my name is Shoshana, I'm from Hawaii, Maui, and I'm having some trouble now. (breathe and shake) I'm addicted to chocolate and the airport shop was closed last night. And I don't have any and I don't think I'm going to make it.

Hut # 10

If anyone has anything, one bite left from a partly eaten candy bar, any sugar or candy from the plane, I'm in hut number 10."
I shook when I took my seat on the floor, revealing my shame and need, to a bunch of strangers, rather, fellow travelers. I mean, this was not a therapy group.
When I went back to my hut later, there was a pile of partially eaten open wrappers of candy in the middle of my bed. I cried.

Moral of the story, what I learned about the Chakras paled in comparison to what I learned about speaking into my emotional truth and the kindness of fellow Journeyers.

Invitation: Take a risk, Custom for you.

Invitation: Valuing Your Gifts...You are the Gift

Years ago I saw an interview on TV of a woman in her '90s. She was asked what her secret was to living such a long and vibrant life. She replied "Ideas. I have a lot of ideas." That stayed with me for decades. I used to identify myself as an "ideas" person, and now I say I'm a Creative.

I'm especially happy because now you are Journeying with me and I've come to know that we are all Creatives. Because of You, I feel received almost instantly in real time. It's not even about the content. I feel received at the level I'm sending. I call that 'Pitcher-Catcher.'

How can you value your own Gifts both to yourself and to the larger community?

Elli says, "I'm valuing my gifts by dedicating my life to spreading the joy of dance in my community and supporting Shoshana in making her dream a reality."

Invitation: Keep an ongoing list of interests you'd like to explore. Like writing topics and pictures you may want to paint or draw.

Sometimes we don't know the source of our interest but it's important to honor what stimulates the mind and write it down for future reference. It has shown up for a reason. Our Soul often speaks indirectly, in symbols, in words, and we might not decipher it's value in the moment that it appears on our list. That's why keeping the list holds value for our creative process.

African Sketchbook

Movement is Key

When I opened my first Center on Halsted Street, I sat down at my desk that first day and racked my brain to come up with my answer to the question, "What do you think Healing is?" What came to me was, "Healing is Movement. Moving from one state to another." I began including movement and breath. Since then I have expanded my definition of healing exponentially.

Still, movement is fundamental to me. All my chairs either rock or roll. I love hammocks, motorcycles (though I don't ride anymore), sports cars, flying (I took flying lessons), hot air balloons.

Elli, my assistant, friend, soul supporter, professional dancer, tech marvel and confidant has brought her version of movement into my Soul Journey. When she enters my house, music is on and we dance first. It's not just her skills and capabilities, we have a heart connection. I LOVE music and I dance every day and have for many years.

For All of You who are Journeying with me on this oh-so-personal and perhaps sometimes Archetypal Journey, I could not do this without You. I feel there is no distance in the heart or the Soul for that matter. We are Journeying together. The right people find each other.

Invitation: Listen to this song by the O'Jays - Love Train

Yesterday, I was listening to this song (Boomers you'll remember this) and started a Conga Line in my house (I live alone) and laughing my butt off.

Snake Rattle

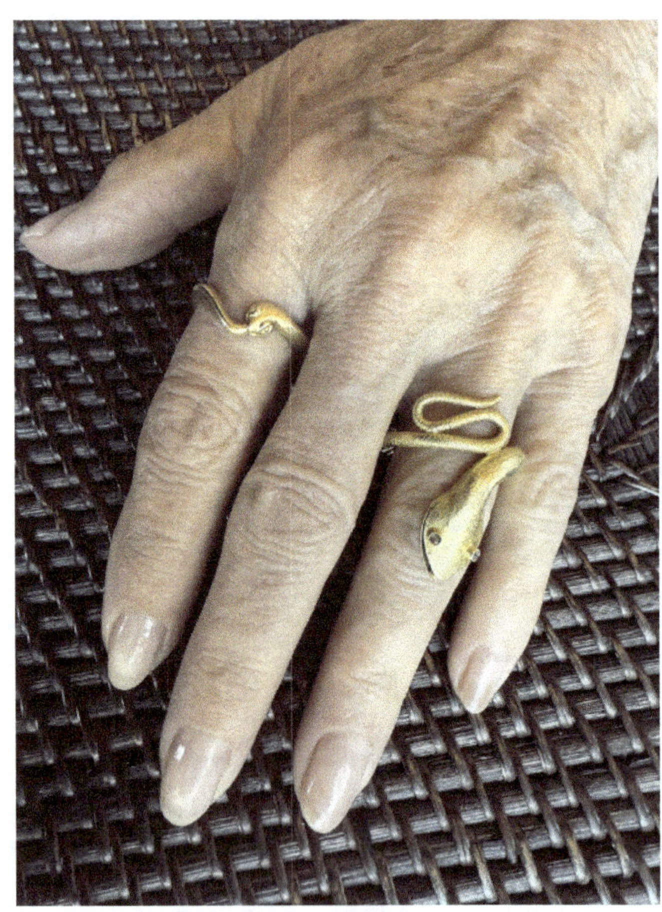

Snake Medicine...The Year of the Snake

What does Snake conjure up for you? Is it a scary feeling or do you love snakes? If it's scary, is it the venom that is scary? Or feeling unprotected from something that can "ambush" your reality and harm you? Or is it the shedding, becoming unknown to another layer or version of yourself? Or none of the above?

Whatever the case, Snake has been brought into our consciousness for the brief moment in eternal time, so shall we take to our creative selves/Souls and invite it in consciously?

Invitation: Do your version of creating Snake. Find a twig or a branch, paint or glue on some eyes, etc. Make a snake out of clay.

The Chinese have brought through some Powerful Medicine with Snake Energy. Bring it through your consciousness and see what it reveals to you and what your relationship to it is.

My Big Dragonfly Drum,
which I painted

Dragonfly Medicine: Journey to the Light

Word went around Chicago that a Female Shaman came to town. She drummed for me and took me on a Journey to find my Power Animal. When the drumming stopped, she said to me, "What animal came for you?" and I said, "All I got was this damn bug." (I'm embarrassed with my behavior.)

She said, "It's medicine is magic. Read about it. Dragonfly is Powerful Medicine." And so I did. And it spoke of the light and I flashed back to my father who used to call me Miss Light. "You just want the world to be Utopia, don't you?" he'd say. And I'd answer, "Yes, yes I do."

There's an imprint there, though I didn't know it at the time. My love of the Stars would come later.

Fast forward to an Ayahuasca Journey where I met Barbara who owned the Dragonfly Ranch on the Big Island. We connected at a deep level and she invited me to come to the Big Island and help her run her beloved Dragonfly Ranch, which I did. (I had been carrying a paper clipping of the Dragonfly Ranch for years in my appointment book. Destiny!)

Invitation: Explore your Power Animal(s) in your Creative Way.

Dragonfly in my Hand

My Needlepoints

Working Dry

As a child, control was the environment I grew up in. Creativity was absent, I mean totally. Professionals were relied on for that. An interior designer was hired to 'decorate' our apartment, restaurants were a daily experience, and my bedroom was decided by mother and her interior decorator. Even my wedding was totally orchestrated by mother and a wedding planner. I never saw the invitations, don't know the colors, mother chose my dress (a puffed-out organza number), which I immediately changed out of after walking down the aisle...into a slinky black pantsuit with mirrored black sandals. I chose nothing...not even my eyeglasses. (I won't show you the picture of me in those white glasses that looked like they belonged to Lily Tomlin when she played 'the Operator' in her comedy sketch.)

So, the bow was pulled back far, and I didn't stay in that disempowered state forever.

Segue...So, paint was out of the question. Water signaled no control, so I "worked dry" as I call it.

I did needlepoints, sweaters, coats and scarves. My needlepoint pillows were left behind when my parents moved.

So I wrote. At age 12, I won an essay contest, "What my American heritage means to me." It was an 8-day all expenses paid trip to Washington DC, with about 75 other students from the Chicago area. No one in my family read my essay or asked me about it. On the trip,

Journeying through Africa

I was chosen to do the daily write-up which was published in the Washington newspaper each day. Even though I've written 8 books and 2 children's stories, nothing has been published. It wasn't until I discovered Facebook (it's immediacy) and You, and Elli, that I felt the personal connection and care that was missing in my writing, bringing me a new imprint. Eternal Gratitude. Pitcher/Catcher, being received at the level you're sending in real time.
Talk about polarities. I identify as a polarity-walker. Recently, I heard one of our top scientists say, "We live in a polarized universe." OK, "Honey, I'm home."

Invitation: Take Creative Risks in the materials that feel right for you in the moment, and in the situation you're in.

Warrior Tending the Sheep

Women at their Dwelling

Women in Ceremony at the Fire at Night

Covid & African Dreaming

When Covid arrived, as they say, "One door closed, another opened."

I first saw pictures of Africa in a Social Studies book when I was 9. It left an imprint. So, when Covid appeared, I took to my art materials and gave my 9-year-old Self the freedom of expression I didn't have an outlet for then.

These four pictures below I call, "African Dreaming," and they have drapes so they represent looking through a window.

I crack up when I look at the one with the sheep with chicken bones for legs, and a branch that came from a tree in Patrick Park where I like to walk. (The branch was found on the ground.) So my invitation is to customize something you may have discarded, be it an idea, or an image, or an exploration...for whatever reason, it wasn't given your full self expression.

IT'S YOUR LIFE! Customize it!

'Children Playing at the Baobab'
The child on the right with black and red checks is gay. (Had to include him.)

Acting (On the Stage and Off)

I took acting classes at a local theater school on Lincoln Avenue in Chicago back in the day. My friend and soul sister, Nancy, and I were chosen for a scene in class from the movie 'The Turning Point' starring Shirley McLaine and Anne Bancroft.

There was a fight scene where they were swinging at each other on a rooftop. Nancy and I were directed to throw a wine glass filled with water in the face of the other acting partner. We did the scene back then and when we reminisce, we can't remember who threw the water in the other one's face. (Cracking up!)

I also took classes at Steppenwolf, so I tried out for Dolly in Hello Dolly at the small acting school where I trained at, and I was chosen. We didn't do the musical version, thank God. Rehearsals went well, I pulled off flamboyant and fun. Take a breath. Opening night, I was jazzed. Our dressing rooms were on the 2nd floor. I was changing and preparing and listening for my cue, when I took a step and missed it and fell down the two flights of stairs. (there was no landing between them in this old rickety building.) Help! I got up and proceeded to go onstage.

For those Baby Boomers who remember Jackie Gleason's show, The Honeymooners, there was an episode when he and Norton were trying to sell a product on TV. In their stage rehearsal, like me, he was fine. Then, when the curtain call came in for him, he knocked over the cardboard wall and went onstage, where Norton was waiting for him to sell their product. His eyes were bulging out of his head, stuttering "Hubba, hubba," making faces, and meandering his way to the counter where he and Norton were going to pitch their 'get rich quick' scheme.

I almost did the female version of that performance. I forgot my lines, was probably in shock from the fall, didn't anticipate the lights being on me and a crowd of people in the seats. I got through it and after the show, Michael, our director, came over and said, "Who were you?" I said, "Michael, I'm so sorry, I forgot to act." Help!

That took care of my theater career. Thank goodness the understudy went on after that. Fast forward, I have issues/performance anxiety which you must have figured out by now. I'm working on it. I know it's roots and I'm telling all the Selves that live inside me, that being myself is good enough.

Invitation: Have a good laugh at something you may have felt embarrassed about.

Making Peace with the Flow

In 1982 I sat in my first Art Therapy class taught by Don Seiden, head of the Department. Fifteen of us sat at a big table with crayons strewn about in the center. After intros, we were asked/invited to make a picture- no content or direction offered. Scared. I had never done this, gone inside and waited for an image.

Well, this is what came out, and I was called to write on the top of it these words, "Making Peace with the Flow."

Where did this come from? No one wrote words on their pictures and at that time I had no clue I was a writer and a lover of words. There was foreshadowing here, big time. Why the drapes? Why my back? Why onstage? Why sitting down? What was Flow? Back then, I didn't know that one's unconscious can appear in one's art. Can I call that Art? Now I say yes, it was self-expression and it had symbols and meaning that I would decipher much later.

So, FLOW. It's a big word now in the collective. Let's just start with breath. How is my breathing? How often am I contracting? What feelings are being revealed, explored, delivered to my consciousness? Am I in FLOW? Hmmm…

Invitation: Draw something without having an image in mind. See what comes out and see what message(s) it has for you.

Water (Flow)

Living in Hawaii, surrounded by water, it came to me, "I want to create a Water Company!" This was back in the '90s where there were only two water companies at the time: Perrier & another. It was a time when we began walking around with water bottles and massage was coming into the collective as well. (I used to think that we were trying to recreate our changing table experiences at an adult level.)

So I made some inquiries, took it pretty far, and my company would be called "Prayer in a Bottle." My vision was to have the water prayed over before it was bottled. A different prayer would be printed on each bottle. At that time, it hadn't occurred to me that each of us could do our own prayers. Duh!

Fate overrode my plan and I left Hawaii for the mainland. What I told myself back then, "I was too horizontal and I needed to get into vertical energy and groundedness." I had experienced what I needed in the Garden of Eden chapter of my life and there is more to come... I got to be imprinted with Flow at a visceral level, floating in the middle of the ocean, sarongs versus fitted clothing, dancing hula. The imprint was huge, being in the womb of the Great Mother!

Invitation: Imagine Your Version of Flow as surrendering and softening no matter what environment you are in.

My Personal Pipe with Wood from Africa, carved by my boyfriend

Pipe Carrier

When I first moved to Santa Fe, I was living in a little Casita off Canyon Road, pretty hidden, when a knock on my door and an elderly, ancient looking woman appeared carrying a very long ceremonial pipe. It seemed like a mirage, out of time. The pipe was longer than my arms, so someone else would have to light it. Long feathers, fur, bone and animal hide adorned this sacred object. It looked bigger than her. She spoke to me very deliberately. "I brought this for you," she whispered. I was in a kind of dream-like shock. No one knew I was here, let alone an ancient woman from a local tribe.

I met her reached-out arms and received the pipe. She said it was 150 years old. After she left, I placed it on my fireplace mantel.

Weeks later, I was invited to a Women's Circle here in town, so I brought my 24" Ceremonial Drum that I bought in Taos and painted a Dragonfly on it. A woman approached me and said, "You are a Pipe Carrier. Come to me for instruction and initiation." So I did.

When it was time for me to bring a Pipe, I brought the big beautiful Pipe that came to me months ago. She said to me, "That is NOT your pipe," emphasizing the NOT. "You need a Personal Pipe."

My boyfriend and I were on our way to Africa. While there, he acquired a piece of wood and carved the stem/ neck of it for me and I bought its pink rose quartz bowl at our local flea market, and then I embellished it.

Many Women's Ceremonies began with that Pipe and its teachings, inhaling our dreams and visions round after round. Years later, before I left Ashland, Oregon, I gave the Ceremonial Pipe to my friend Steve who did Sweat Lodges each week with Native People. I heard he died shortly after I left and I'm so glad he had a chance to Journey with the Sacred Pipe.

Dumás Pére, French Cooking School

A gourmet French Cooking School, Dumás Pére, opened up in a large warehouse in the suburbs of Chicago. It was a one year program and I was interested. There were fifteen kitchens, fourteen people were opening restaurants, and me, who grew up in restaurants and didn't know how to cook.

The first lesson was to make stock and we were given homework to go to different neighborhoods, gather ingredients (there were no big supermarkets then) boil all the stuff in a big stock pot and bring in our stock in the form of two ice cubes to class to finish the remainder of the recipe. My huge pot boiled all the way down and I was left with just enough liquid to squeeze out two ice cubes which I brought to class.

Before Chef John entered our space, I approached some of the other students with my bright idea that maybe only one person could do the homework for all and we could take turns. They were hearing none of this, and my tail was between my legs.

On the week we did brioche, we had a lot of sitting around and waiting for the dough to rise, so I tried to bamboozle the gal in the kitchen next to me to put our containers of dough in the back seat of my car and go to Neiman's (down the road) and have lunch, shop, etc, while our dough was rising. We covered our dough and left the car for a little lunch and shopping. When we returned, the dough was sprawled out all over the backseat. The two of us were like Lucy & Ethel, punching in the dough back into the bowls.

It was a one year program, and after graduation I made a special meal at home: Duck L'Orange, Swirled Cheesecake and I can't remember what else. A few friends were invited to attend and I got a standing ovation. That was the only meal I made from a year of that program. What I learned was how demanding and involved and precise French Cooking is.

P.S. And now you can buy Mirepoix at Trader Joes, all chopped up and ready to go for a few dollars. Progress?

Invitation: Cook a creative meal, have fun and share it with someone, or cook with another, a recipe you desire to try out.

For extra fun, for the women: You can wear your cute one piece apron naked and let the ties in back cover the middle of your butt. It's sexy.

Sweat Lodge Ceremony

When I told my clients in Chicago I was moving to Santa Fe to take myself on as a client, they were sad, and I wanted to give them a parting gift. A Sweat Lodge Ceremony came to mind. The men's movement had one of its first Centers in Chicago, so I went there to seek support. Upon entering their office I asked, "Can you help me? I would like to bring my women to your facility on North Avenue to have a sweat lodge. Is this possible?" Agreement was given, though no women had entered the space prior. I let it be known that there would be some customizing from Native Traditions, who honor women by having them not enter when 'on their flow.' To me, honoring means front row seats. A water-pourer was offered to assist.

Asking women of my different groups and private clients to meet each other and get naked together back in 1993 was, shall we say, unthinkable. And yet it happened. More than twenty participated. We had a circle in the courtyard first, then undressed and made a procession into the Lodge, which had been heated up and ready for us. As we took our seats and began to chant and speak our dreams into being, we heard the sound of drums. The men from the Center surprised us and gathered around the Lodge on the outer and drummed for us, a Sacred Moment I'm sure we will always remember.

Invitation: Imagine yourself as part of that Ceremony.

Driver's Seat

When I announced to my clients I was moving to Santa Fe, one man came forth and said he would like to drive me. I thought it over and said, "Yes."

Among other things, I needed to exchange my car from a fancy one to a red Jeep with a bra. (You know, the flap on the front) She was a girl.

Alan and I took off with him driving. He loved Santa Fe as well and had been there many times. We enjoyed the drive, imagining the next stages of our lives, and when we got to the border of New Mexico, I asked him to pull over and to switch seats with me, "I want to be in the Driver's Seat of my life when I enter into New Mexico." And we did.

Invitation: What does being in the Driver's Seat of your life mean to you? Imagine and Customize.

One of My Favorite Churches

I pulled over on the side of the road with my watercolors rather than taking a photograph. It feels more personal to me when I can see my own hand's expression.

My Antler Doll and Rock Doll

My Peruvian Doll

Doll Making

I never had a doll. As a child, I saw two girls 'playing' with their dolls and I recall thinking they are talking for their dolls and then putting them down and changing their clothes. This is madness! I didn't know what 'play' was.

In my forties in Chicago I saw an ad for a Doll Making Workshop. So I enrolled. I had made my own version of dolls, made out of rocks and antlers, nothing soft (I didn't know what softness was.)

At the class, we were given a doll to embellish. Most of the women worked on their doll all day, I made one doll after another until there were eight dolls, all from different cultures. The teacher came over to me and asked me a question that still lingers somewhere inside me...stopped me in my tracks. "Do you think you have to create everything in your life?" I answered, "Yes, yes I do." And that question, the right question, speaks volumes to me. I do feel I want to create my Version of a life, perhaps the one I didn't get to live early on.

Then, I created my own doll-making workshops for women. As they were working on their dolls, I read Clarissa Pinkola Estes story Vasalisa the Wise, a story about a doll named Vasalisa from her best selling book, Women Who Run with the Wolves.

I have come to call my relationship to life as the Journey of my Creative Soul.
More than the expression of painting a nice picture on a canvas, Creativity, to me, is the capacity to express ideas, thoughts, feelings and wonderment in our own Customized Version, in our own Customized Ways.

My Creative Soul did not identify with the roles that our culture offered the feminine archetype in the shape of commercial dolls. Having said that, for those who did bond with a doll, the invitation is to retrieve a memory of that experience that touches your heart & write about it.

Maasai Dolls from Africa
Large beaded doll in the center, my first doll, I bought for myself for my 40th Birthday.

Medicine Wheel Ceremony

When I had to have an emergency hysterectomy, my friends appeared at the hospital and brought rocks that they placed on my chakras with tape and performed a ceremony on my body. I asked the doctor, a woman, to save my uterus so that I could pick it up at the lab and keep it in my freezer until I was ready to create a medicine wheel and bury it in the ground...my womb to the womb of the Great Mother.

We put up a teepee first. The day arrived for the ceremony, forty people were invited with the instruction to bring a big rock and we would build a circle (medicine wheel) with all of our rocks. My friend Fidel, Native American, sang traditional songs to call the Circle into being. We went around the circle, each telling a story related to birth and the Great Mother. Then my boyfriend dug a hole in the center and I took my womb out of the freezer and then buried it. I remember saying, "I thought this was my womb, but in this moment I see it is only an organ. My womb is in my heart."

As I write this, I am having an awareness, a flashback, that I didn't have at that time. Perhaps on some level, the burial was what I never had when I lost my baby who died in the 9th month of pregnancy and who I carried 3 weeks more in my body til I naturally delivered her. There was no Ceremony for her back then. Some things happen in their right time.

Womb Rattles

I signed on for a clay class (on a wheel making pots) right after my hysterectomy, but when I walked into the class, I just didn't 'feel it.' I wanted to work directly with my hands, not a machine. So I asked the instructor if it would be all right if I could take some clay and go to the back of the room and see what wanted to be birthed. She said yes (When we allow and leave space for our Creative Soul to appear, it knows.)

Anyhow, I had made pots before on the wheel in Chicago at the Lill Street Gallery. So I kneaded the clay in my hands until it softened a bit, and then it started to form into something that looked like a brain. While the dozen or so in the class were busy pulling up pots on their wheels, I was looking at these forms that started to look like wombs. After cutting them in half and scooping the clay out of the centers, it came to me - I was making a replacement on an unconscious level of the womb I had just buried.

The soul speaks in different languages, which I have come to call our Creative Soul.
Mine needed an outlet to replace feelings that wanted to be seen & honored.

I made 12 of them and gave 11 of them away. They were fired in the kiln, and when they came out I filled them with small crystals in the hole I had placed on their underside. Then my hands made snakes like a child does, and I placed a snake on top of each. WOMB RATTLES! Didn't know what they were until they were finished.

Invitation: When faced with a life-changing event, take to your materials and pen, and make a space for what the Soul wants to express and reveal in its own Language.

Womb Rattle

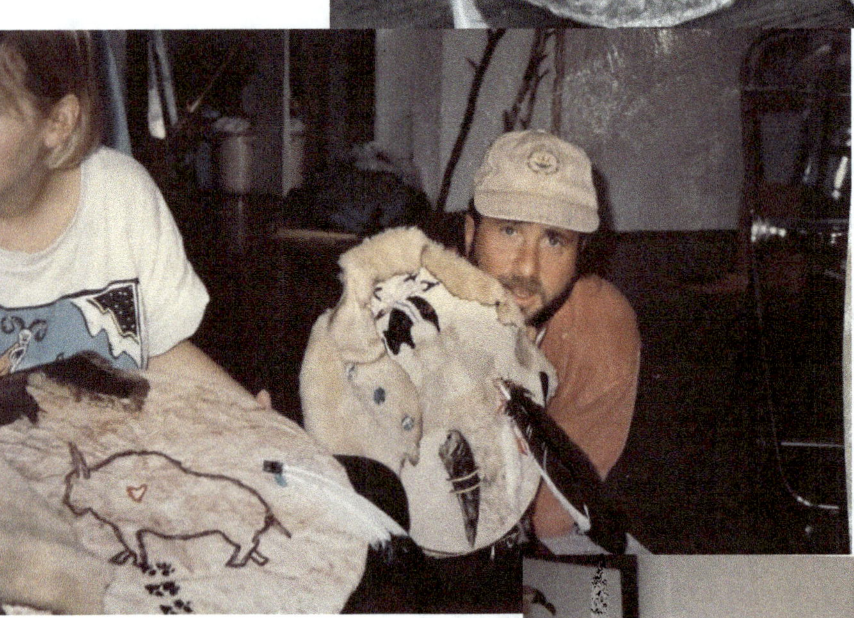

Shields

I had made a series of shields a long time ago, though I can't remember what their themes were (aging!). I brought the idea to one of my groups (both men and women together for the first time) and off we went. (You can get the stretchers/hoops at a craft store and add the canvas to it.)

I loved seeing the interaction of masculine and feminine energies together, respect and interest were present. Creating together in a form - shields - that was traditionally used for protection, transformed it into the realm of a sacred message that revealed something personal of each of their Creative Souls.

Invitation: If you feel inspired to this form, Customize (my favorite word in life) Your Version

Masks

There were many workshops making masks at the Center, and this one stands out. It was the one where we included an already-formed men's group. It took place at my third Center, a two-story loft that was a prior ballroom in its past incarnation. It was where I held workshops and big groups (and later moved into after my divorce).

All went well with the intros and pairing-up, and then when the water and special tape came out (the medical kind used for casts) and when the men began placing the tape over the women's mouths, ancient memories of men silencing women got dislodged and we stopped and dealt with those feelings.

None of us had predicted that theme would surface, I certainly didn't. It added another dimension to the power of art to awaken our Soul's imprints.

Needless to say, that experience brought deep intimacy into the room and into the process.

Invitation: Think about when you feel you have to wear a mask.

Tribe

Long before I went to Africa in this lifetime, a woman in one of my women's groups, proposed to the group that she wanted all of us to wear a necklace as a symbol of our group. All agreed. Then she brought in an image of an African symbol for fertility. We loved it. She found a jeweler in town to make this Sacred Disc (they included me) - so this is the symbol. And I cherish it, and still wear mine.

Invitation: if this speaks to you and you have a friend or a tribe that is Soul-Connected, perhaps you may be inspired to create your own version of Your Tribe.

African Symbol for Fertility

Feathered Pipe Ranch, Montana

I was led to attend a workshop experience on Shamanism at Feathered Pipe Ranch, Helena, Montana. Our group met on this sacred land, each in our own tepee. Every night, we joined with the Blackfeet Indians for a fire circle. Their presence invited the sacredness to our experience.

I wanted to have something personal to offer the fire. There were no art materials so I took my canvas bag, went to the kitchen, got a scissors, cut it up, used lipstick to 'paint' an image onto the canvas, found four long sticks, tied it to the sticks and made my own shield.

At nightfall we gathered around the fire and danced in circle around it to the drum beat. I threw my shield into the fire and one of the men in our group stepped into the fire to retrieve it for me. He didn't know my gesture was intentional. I was touched and thanked him, and then got a second chance to toss it in again.

During the day, we all wandered around the grounds. I saw a young girl ride by on her horse. I stopped her and we chatted. I asked her if she could bring a second horse with her tomorrow so we could ride together...and she did. I really felt the blessing of this gift as we rode together freely in the woods of Montana.

Returning to Chicago and to the high rise I was living in, was such a confining juxtaposition of who I really am/was. From sleeping on the ground in a tepee, to pushing buttons in the elevator...my inside certainly did not meet my outside. That theme followed me for much of my life in Chicago.

Invitation: Have a look at the relationship of the inner and outer selves.

Me on My Horse King

"Trust Shoshana, Trust"

When I turned 60, I wanted to start the next decade on the back of a horse at sunrise on top of a mountain. So I called Bishop's Lodge here in Santa Fe and arranged for a wrangler to meet me at the stables at 6:00 AM. The day arrived and he saddled up two horses and we "picked" (a word that cowboys use to meander without a trail) our way up to the top of a local mountain.

There was a place where we had to take a little jump. Oh no! I'm not going to do that! I had never jumped while on a horse before. Falls, yes. In Chicago, my neighbor and I used to race horses at her barn on the border of Illinois and Indiana. There was a forest preserve nearby. One day, with snow and ice on the ground I took a fall with my horse half on top of me, because she and I were racing on ice. Cra-cra.

Back to the wrangler. So I said to him, a young man, "I have to get off! I'll get right back on after he takes the jump." He said in a loud and angry voice, "Trust, Shoshana, Trust!" I pleaded with him, "Really, I'll get right back on." Again, "Trust, Shoshana, Trust!" he ordered me.
I took a breath and let the horse do his thing.

It was an amazing sunrise, and when I returned home, I sat down and contemplated, "What am I supposed to trust? Life? Love? Myself?" and I wrote a piece on it back then.

Over the years I can't help but contemplate those words that were delivered in a loud tone that penetrated me far deeper than the moment. My current answer to that question now is, yes, yes and yes.

Invitation: Where are you at in your relationship to Trust? And, what is it that is calling you to Trust?

evian

Power Sticks & Talking Sticks

I Invited one of the women's circles to create Power Sticks and Talking Sticks. They could choose which one felt right for them; a small one to use for sitting in circle, or a larger one for walking with in the woods. I demonstrated the Talking Stick I was working on (pictured here) and which I used at Fire Ceremonies. One of the women didn't have a Power Stick and I made a quick decision to give my big one to her. It was a real tall one, like me, and she was happy to receive it.

A few years ago, I found a big twisted stick on one of my walks here, near the Community College. I painted it white, put a rubber tip on the bottom, and used it when I was dealing with Spinal Stenosis. So many people stopped me to comment on the stick. In fact, a couple asked me about the stick one morning at a local restaurant, and then invited me to have breakfast with them. They are now dear friends and like family. Though I don't use it now, it is personal and sacred to me on my Journey.

Invitation: If you feel called, paint and embellish a stick, even if you don't use it. There's a reason it's called a Power Stick.

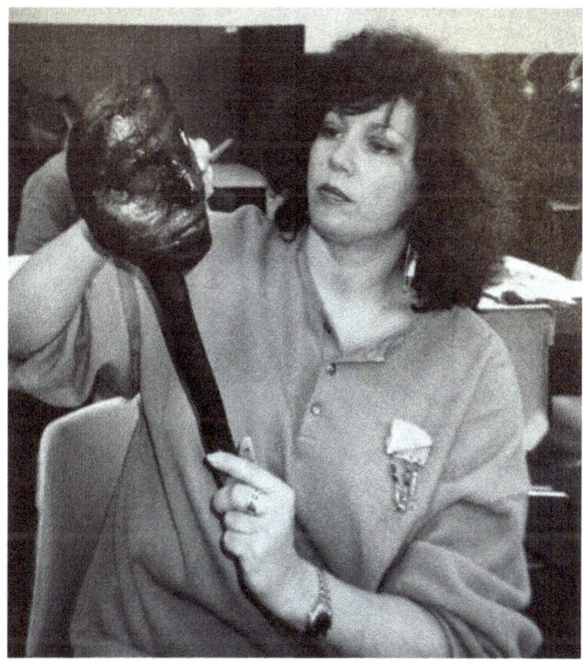

President of Kenya

**Young Women braiding
my hair in their Dwelling**

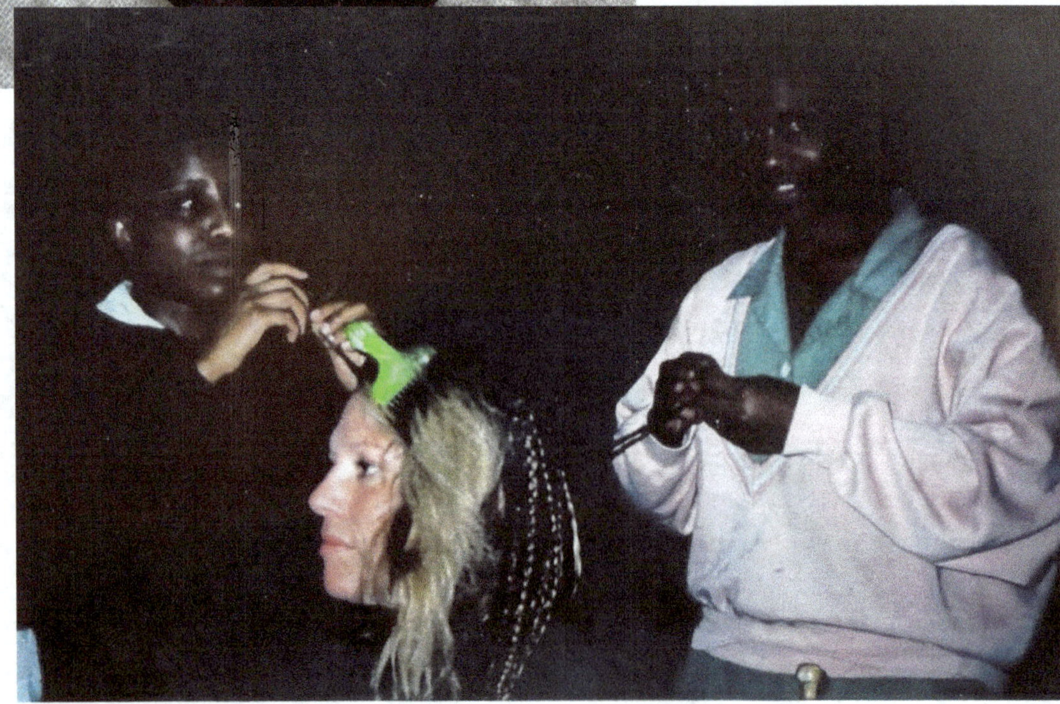

Africa, Egypt and Nile Full Moon

It just so happened I was floating down the Nile on a Full Moon. When my boyfriend and I traveled to Egypt and Africa, the first thing I did upon entering Egypt was buy a snake cane at one of the outdoor stands. I didn't know why, because consciously I was afraid of snakes back then. The tour we were on was planned in advance and we ended up floating down the Nile on a Full Moon. Destiny!

It was lined up by Sources I was not conscious of at the time. In fact, the last thing I did when getting on the plane for our return trip back to the states was hand my snake cane to someone at the airport. Mistake!

In Kenya, I couldn't get enough of Maasai beads. My Soul was definitely connected to that tribe. They welcomed me in such precious and intimate ways. The women took me into one of their dwellings and spent a good long time braiding my hair. The men took me into their dwellings and we sat together for another good long time. A part of me felt familiar with their culture, not seeing differences, seeing 'meeting places.'

Here in Santa Fe, we have an International Folk Art Market every year where people from countries all over the world bring their wares/gifts for our community. It is amazing to see the different cultures wearing their local garb walking through our Plaza.

I was blessed to meet the President of Kenya, pictured here, giving a talk at our travel bookstore. He brought Africa to us. I remember my ceremony with the Maasai women who took off their necklaces and placed them around my neck as I placed our local turquoise necklaces around theirs (I brought 12 turquoise necklaces from our Flea Market, to Africa, hoping to place them on Sisters from the other side of the world.) I was so honored to be welcomed into their tribe.

I wore their necklaces for a few days, not wanting to take off the feeling of initiation that they carried, however, they smelled bad and I wrestled with the notion of washing off the 'blood sweat and tears of Africa' down a sink in the lodge. I did eventually soak them in the sink and cried at the same time.

In Egypt I wore a camel's teeth necklace and eventually took to washing it as well.

Invitation: Trust who you identify with

Full Moon - Haleakala, Maui

Hale (house of) Akala (the Sun)

In the center of Maui there's a very old volcano, hasn't erupted in 150 years, called Haleakala. There's a winding road that takes about 2-3 hours to the top, depending on what part of the island you're coming from. I loved the drive as I always loved to feel like I'm in the driver's seat of my life.

You could see horses, cows, flower farms and then the terrain changed and it looked like you were in a desert at the end of the world. It was otherworldly...coming from the lush and moist terrain of Mother Maui. You could see the coast line, like on a map. I loved the perspective. When I lived there, maybe 6-8 people would be up there on a Full Moon. Now, there are busses, tours and tickets needed on the internet 3 weeks in advance (no words).

Back when I was there, the feeling on a Full Moon was Sacred. Those who gathered would 'tone' together and wait for the Magic.

A little science...on a Full Moon, you are literally standing between the sun and moon, one in front of you and the other behind. And because the sun is 400 times larger than the moon and the moon is 400 times closer than the sun, they both look the same size. And because Haleakala is over 10,000 feet high, they are literally lower than where you stand. So, I was standing right in the middle of those energies. Magic!

This experience was a Wonder of my life...like being in Outer Space.

It was 1999 and word on the planet was that computers may shut everything down on New Year's. I called my father in Florida on NYE and said to him, "Dad, if all goes down, I want to say goodbye, after all 'I'm floating in the middle of the Ocean'." Without skipping a beat he said, "If you go up 50,000 miles, we're all floating in the middle of the Ocean."

Surprised at his perspective I replied, "Dad, I think that's the most spiritual thing you've ever said." Now, his perspective is even higher than that.

Invitation: Look Up! (More on that later)

The Three Great Pillars of the Temple

Mosaics of the Dolphins

Temple of Knossos, CRETE

On the island of Crete, there is a Temple called the Temple of Knossos, considered the oldest city in Europe. It carries with it a famous story of a Minotaur and the Labyrinth. The Minotaur had the body of a man and the head of a bull, and the Labyrinth is a maze that imprisoned the Minotaur.

Our culture is familiar with other Greek Myths: Pandora's box, The Trojan War, and the Minotaur in the Labyrinth is right up there. To me, it spoke to feeling trapped and not knowing which way to go.

When I saw the mosaics on the temple walls it triggered a childhood memory of my love for those little tiles, not knowing their source and the fascination of that myth.

Invitation: Is there a myth or fairytale that lives inside of you and speaks to a theme or archetype in your life?

Entry Ticket to the Temple of Knossos

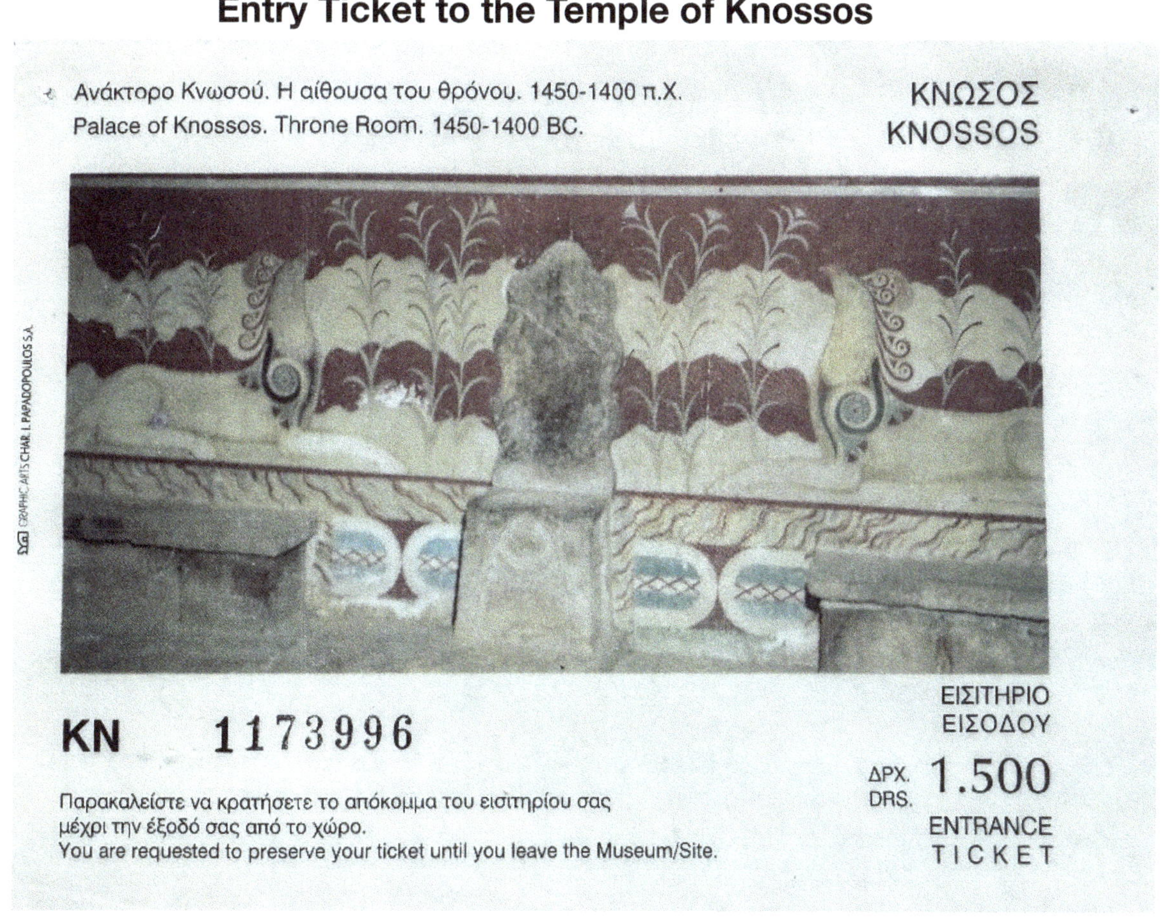

Istanbul

Pulling into the harbor of Istanbul with the sound of ancient bells ringing, takes one out of time. The boat docked and we went directly to Hagia Sophia, the Grand Mosque, where prayers are held five times a day. Outside the doors are racks of thousands of shoes, capacity inside is 18,000, and the entire floors are covered with overlapping carpets. Folded over into prayer position on the floor were thousands of men. The women were in a separate area. These images are pictures that come to life with sound, smell, frequency of prayer in ancient architecture meeting modern lifestyle.

Such a polarity between life and lifestyle - these are five dimensional pictures of literally walking into another time and space. It's alive. I'm painting a picture with words.

Invitation: Imagine a Sacred Moment in your life, with all the dimensions that it stirs for you.

Sketchbook Pic of Grand Mosque

Two Earring Designs and Necklace

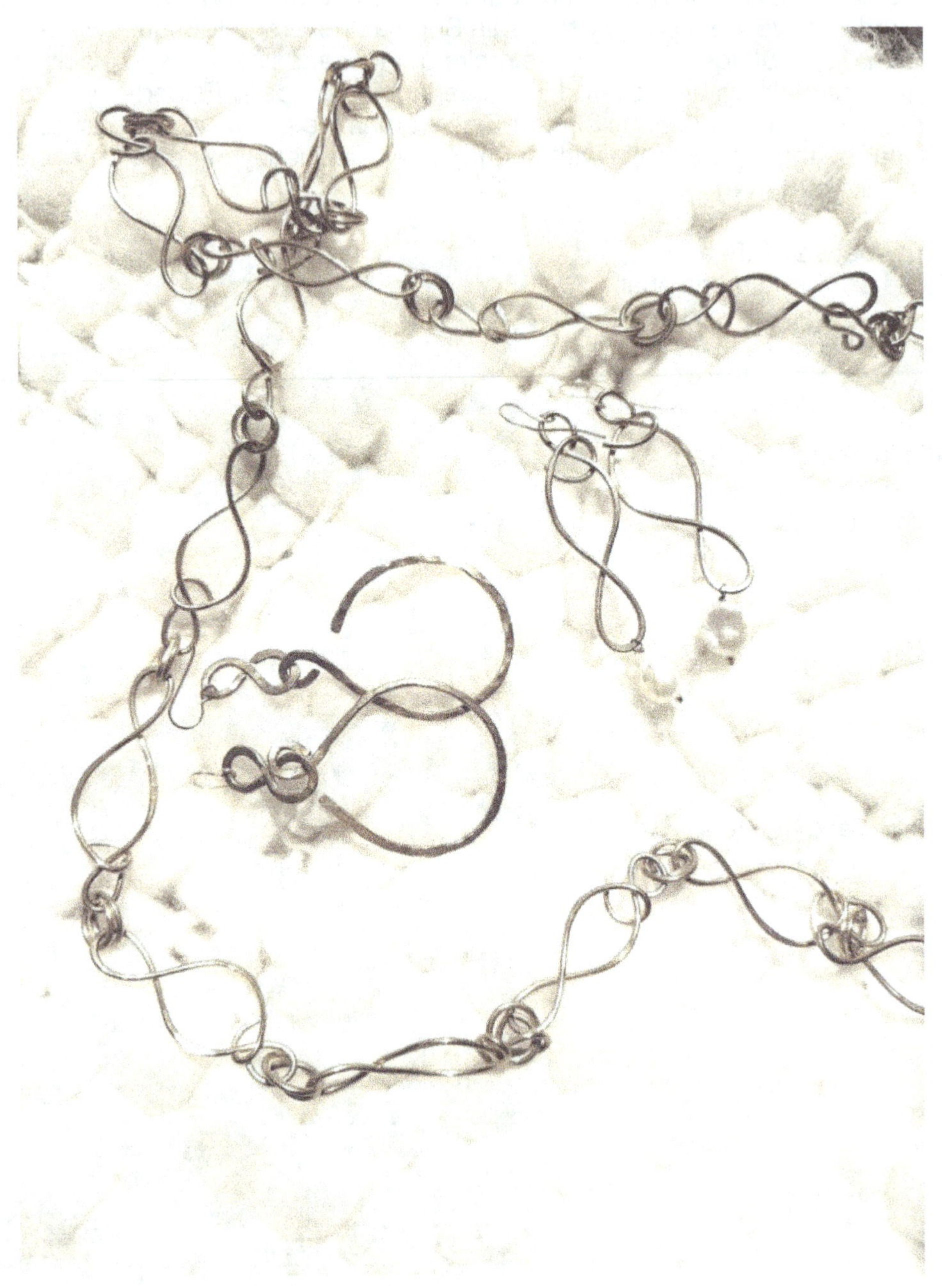

The Blue Bead

When I moved back to Santa Fe (the second time living here) my finances were low. I got a job at a local bead store, helping behind the counter. Lots of fun people came in along with teachers who taught classes on various forms of beading.

One of the teachers invited me to sit in on a class. They were making intricate designs with microscopic beads and threads that only a spider could navigate. Not me, though I loved what they were creating. The teacher and I took to each other, and I asked her if she had bigger and thicker wire or metal I could use. She said, "Yes, in my studio in Albuquerque." So we set up an appointment.

There was a bead, however, that stood out to me in the store. It was Greek Islands blue, with gold on it. Something about it stopped me in my tracks. It was as if a doorway opened into ancient memories of Egypt, Greece and faraway lands and times. I bought the bead, not knowing why.

One thing led to another. The teacher's studio was huge and had lots of beaded designs and spools of gold wire in various sizes. I said, "I'd like to use the big wire, the biggest one." She said, "It's too big, you couldn't handle it." (I had to try.)

"Do you have a hammer?" I asked. She provided me with one, and I pounded out these earrings. Since I knew nothing of how things attached, or any way to make it happen, I had to figure out a design that could match my beginner level jewelry-making.

We were both amazed. The energy and frequency running through me was too much to manage and I jumped off the stool to run outside to jump and scream. I was flooded with Creative Energy.

Then I continued on and made a collection, which sold at the top jewelry store on Canyon Road and at Body of Santa Fe.

Invitation: Trust your own style and ways of Creating that are Custom to you.

My Watercolor of Mother

Taking to the paints brought me closer to my feelings for my mother

Backs

Living in Santa Fe with a significant Native American population and nineteen Pueblos in the surrounding areas, the Native presence brings a powerful imprint to all those who make a stop here at the end of the Santa Fe Trail. It's a living history. Wagon Trains passed through and the adobe architecture is everywhere. I live in an adobe home now, modern, yet I have lived in many others.

There is a sensitivity to taking photographs of the Native Americans who beautifully wear their cultural heritage in their clothing and jewelry. Gorgeous, ancient, Sacred, their presence creates a culture here and one can't help but want to photograph. However, it's as if a piece of their Soul is trying to be captured as some kind of souvenir. No bueno! It's not done here.

Back to backs. With our cell phones clicking photos of everything and selfies commonplace, and presentation (being camera-ready) so much of the norm of modern-day culture, things have certainly changed.

Which leads to its polarity...fronts. "Front lawn living," which is how I grew up. Everything was placed on how it looks from the outer. What you presented was all that mattered, which I call 'packaging.'

I grew up with rigid guidelines about 'presentation': "Put a smile on your face!" "Don't let anyone see what's inside!" What the f*** was inside anyway? Undealt-with feelings that didn't fit into the superficial ways people presented themselves.

Being from the Baby Boomer Generation, I wanted a real picture of mother, and funny, she seemed softer, more vulnerable from the back. It was her last picture. She passed away shortly afterwards.

There are many perspectives to consider in life. There's the hidden, the interior, the back, the front.

Invitation: Imagine what it would feel like if somebody wanted to take a picture of your back.

"Misty"

When I first heard the song Misty, by Johnny Mathis, I fell in love with the song. I play it almost every day, still. When mother signed my brother and I up for piano lessons, I knew what I wanted. I wanted to play Misty like a pro.

The teacher arrived and went over the lessons. (Very primary and I had no interest in learning them.) I told him about my love of the song Misty, and asked him if we could skip all the preliminaries and could he teach me all that I needed to be able to play my favorite song. I guess I was persuasive or what other people have called me, relentless.

I learned the chords, I could make the runs, and push came to shove I could play it pretty darn well, go figure!

Fast forward, I'm teaching at a Chicago inner city school and I became friends with a woman named Fran. One day, she said to me, "I'd like you to meet my cousin." He came over and seemed to take to me. He was way older than I was. One day he said, "I'd like to take you to meet my family." Off we went to his sister's house. During a tour of the house we went into the basement where an old piano was sitting against the wall. He looked at me and said, "Do you play?" I hesitated and then he said, "Can you play Misty?" (Hand to Bible) I played beautifully my only song. He was smitten as he loved piano bars. We were married shortly after.

Moral of the story...Customize, do it your way.

P.S. Sarah Vaughan - Misty (Sweden, 1964) Fabbb
and Johnny Mathis anytime, anyplace, anywhere

Sketchbook Images

Memphis
Sphinx, Cairo
Amazing juxtaposition of fertile land & desert.
Land of the living next to the land of the dead
Step Pyramid
Oldest pyramid in Egypt

1st piece of architecture in ancient Egypt.
Here, cross-legged, in the shape of a pyramid,
I breathed through the chakras - connecting
each one w/ the energy of ancient Egypt.
It was easy, familiar, the sounds, smells,
earth & sky. Perhaps I've done this before.
▲ = symbol of eternity & everlasting life.
We buy a carpet for our meditation practice
Together we gather things for our altar.
Great Pyramids, Cheops

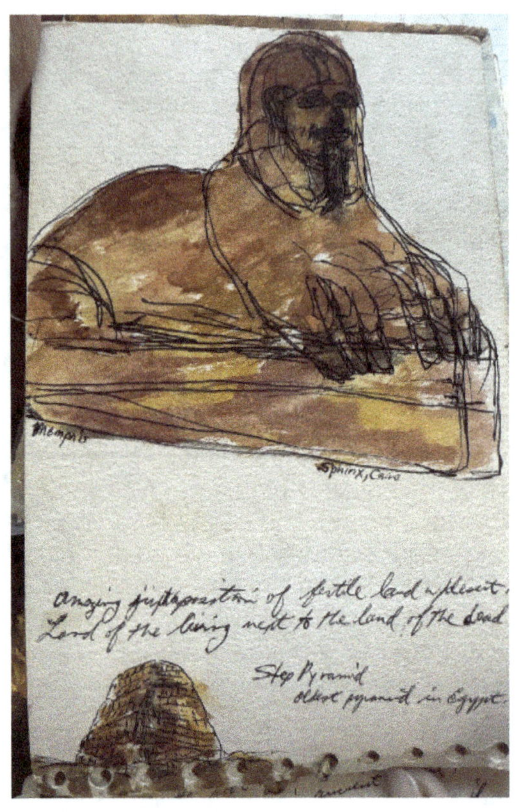

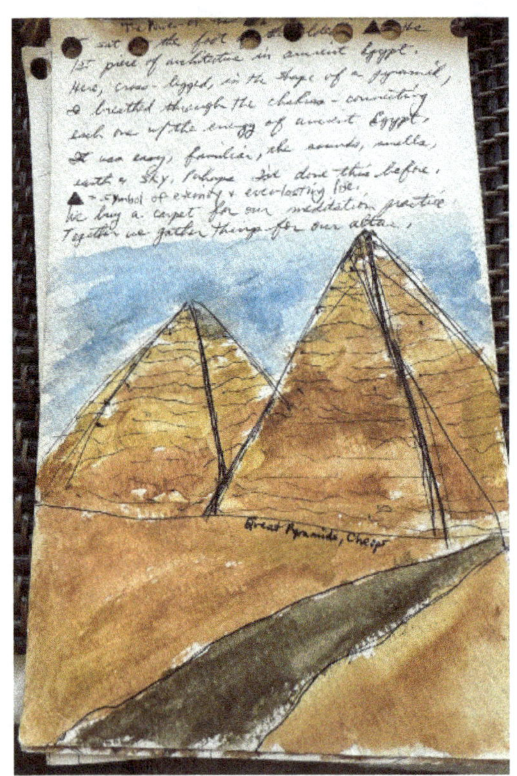

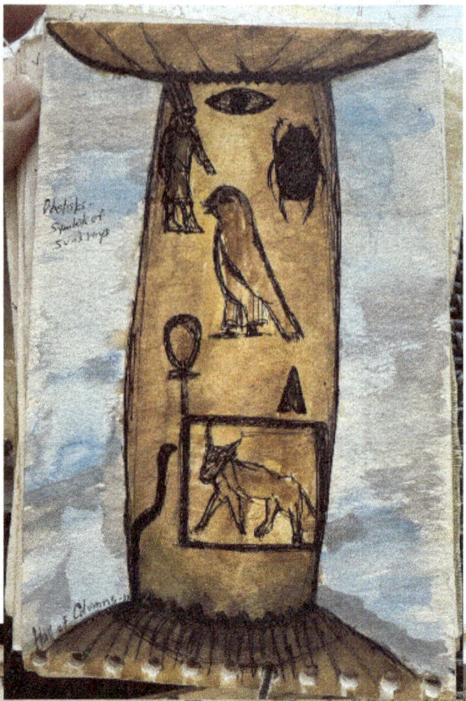

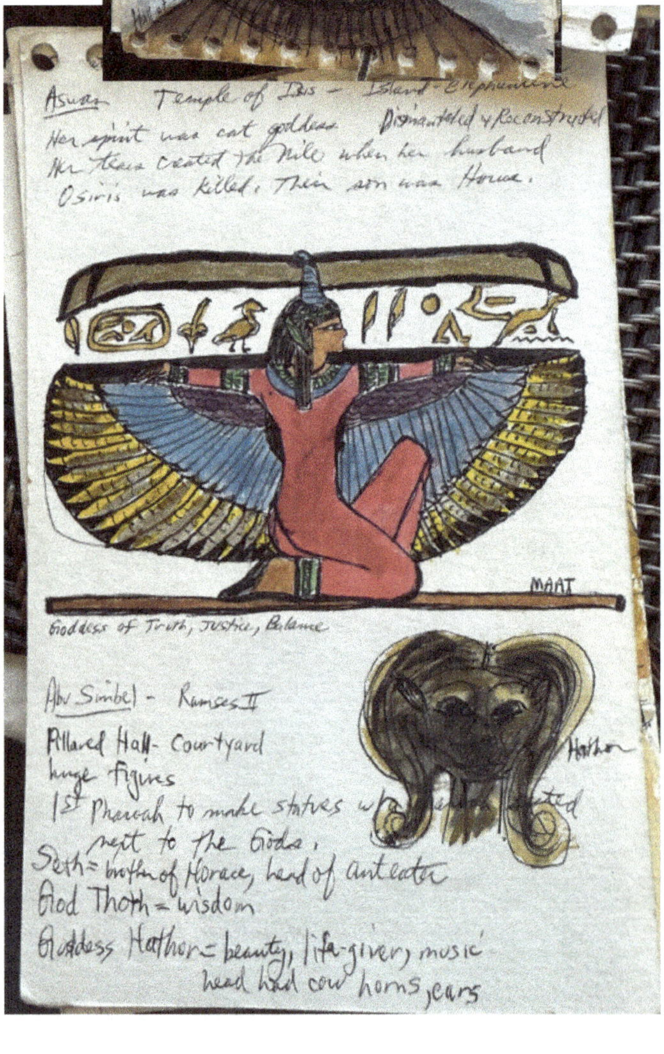
Aswan Temple of Isis - Island - Elephantine
Her spirit was cat goddess Dismantled & Reconstructed
Her tears created the Nile when her husband
Osiris was killed. Their son was Horus.
MAAT
Goddess of Truth, Justice, Balance
Abu Simbel - Ramses II
Pillared Hall - Courtyard
huge figures
1st Pharoah to make statues
next to the Gods.
Seth = brother of Horace, head of anteater
God Thoth = wisdom
Goddess Hathor = beauty, life-giver, music
head had cow horns, ears
Hathor

Sketchbook

Spring is in the air and as long as we're called to go outside let's bring our inner artist outside as well. This 5 1/2 x 8 1/2 sized sketchbook accompanied me through Egypt and Africa. Small watercolor paper was easy to manage. Don't forget to take your Water Bottle along with watercolor paints. Quick and innocent, these images touch me in ways that modern technology can't come close. Choose a bag that's lightweight and mobile and waterproof.

Invitation: Do your version and have fun!

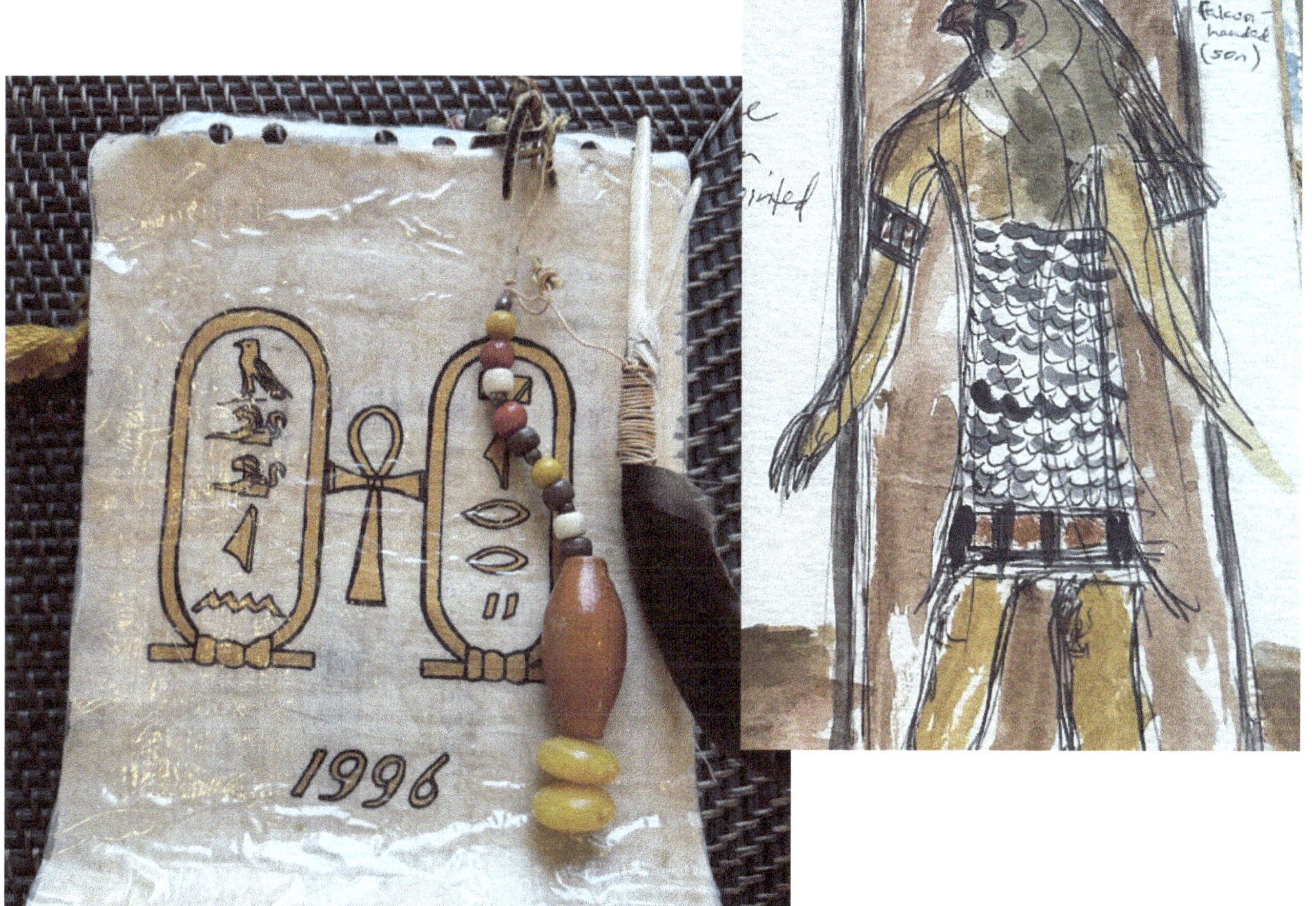

Camels in Israel

I ran into two camels in Israel, one at the Wailing Wall, the other in the wide open desert. At the beginning of the big piazza of the Wailing Wall, which is a piece of the old temple, stood a boy with his camel. I approached him. "What's your camel's name?" I inquired. "Michael Jackson," he responded. We had a fun moment together.

Fast forward to a Santa Fe writing workshop. I was partnered with a man named Stuart, who later became a friend. We were to read to each other the opening of a writing we were working on. He went first. The opening line of his mystery novel, which took place in Egypt and Israel began, "And his name was Michael Jackson." I squealed out loud, "You met the camel Michael Jackson?" I asked, practically jumping out of my seat. "Yes, at the Wailing Wall." "Me too!" I screeched with joy.

Well, that was it, we were kindred spirits. In years to come, we both moved to Maui and became writing partners there.

The second camel that I crossed paths with was when I was in the desert of Israel with tour busses that stopped at a big tent in the middle of nowhere, where we were served some ancient drink - some sort of of tea.

Two camels were standing there, saddled up with kilim rugs and all. I knew my butt was gonna be on one of them. I dashed off to stand next to a camel and someone helped me on. Having ridden horses, I thought I could pull it off on this old animal. Well, did he show me. I gave him a kick and he took off. Let me tell you, a camel's gait is not like a horse's. Those amazing images of camel lines in profile walking slowly on top of sand dunes was not what this camel had in mind for 'our ride.'

He took off and ran his butt off, going absolutely nowhere. There was beige 360 degrees. He was not going back to any barn, as they say. I think I was screaming because he/we were out of control. Finally, he stopped and turned around. I was on a runaway camel and the Lone Ranger was not riding shotgun to pull us over and rescue me. My nervous system went from barely a pulse in the sweltering heat, to almost needing resuscitation.

That did not stop me from riding another camel in Turkey, but this time I was well-behaved.

Reaching for the Stars

I was always reaching...reaching for the right lipstick, the right handbag, the right man. I was told that I'd stand in my crib and reach my arms out and call out, "Take-a-me." There was something higher, something more, and one day I came to know I wasn't reaching high enough...and I began Reaching for the Stars.

I was living in Ashland, and it was around 10 at night and I felt a pulling in my chest. It came with a call to go outside, which I did. I looked up and Arcturus was directly overhead. It felt like there might be a connection. Personal events that happened the next day around Arcturus were off the charts. I wrote a book about it called Reaching for the Stars, never published like the 7 other books. Anyhow, I couldn't deny the pull, the connection, especially when I had encounters on Maui with Spika and Vega. When they appeared in the expanse of blackness of the beautiful Maui sky I'd wave to them as friends would, and knew there was some connection.

Over time, 8 constellations and stars appeared with messages telling me which chakras they wanted to be placed in. They became my Galactic Team, supporting the 7 chakras and then Scorpius appeared and instructed me to place him in my back...three stars across the shoulders, the hook going down my back forming the tail I always felt was missing. "I've got your back," was his message. Stars and constellations showing up in my chakras, unbelievable, unplanned, unimaginable, even one planet appeared with a personal message.

I feel blessed to be in relationship to celestial beings, energies, and messages.

Invitation: If you're called, the relationship begins with a connection to one star. Go outside one evening and look up. You don't have to know any of the stars. Just look at one star, any star, for a good minute or two and then see if you feel that that star is looking back at you.
Without that feeling of connection, there is no relationship. That's where it begins. See if you feel that there is a presence.

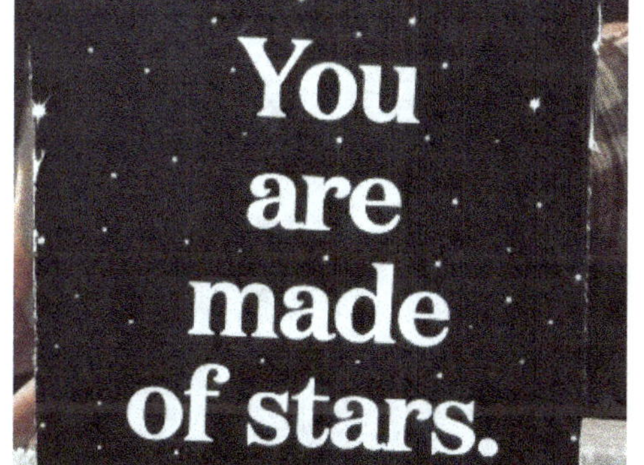

If you're called, the next step is to get a star chart and a small flashlight.
What's amazing about the night sky is that all countries on the earth agree on the top 88 constellations. They don't take a couple stars from one and make a new constellation. They may call them different names, for example in Maui, we call Scorpius 'Maui's Hook.'
Countries can't agree on Earth on hardly anything, but we can agree on the realm of the sky!

Omos - Tribe in Ethiopia

Years ago, I was keeping a list of things I wanted to write about, and on it I had written, "There's something about Ethiopia." It's the country just north of Kenya and it's been said that it's the most isolated country...not in miles, in customs.

Perhaps it was because Queen She-Ba, was the famous Queen of Ethiopia and I grew up with a summer home in Wisconsin named She-Ba for Sherri (my birth name) and my younger brother Barry. A big red & white sign hung over our door with She-Ba written on it, so it was in my memory bank this lifetime as well.

The Omo tribe is from Ethiopia and one of my favorite books is a picture book of that tribe.

Perhaps it was their free relationship to the body, naked, adorned differently each day by dipping into the river and a fellow member of the tribe would 'paint' with mud a design on them, adding branches and flowers, and to me this moved me more than Fashion Week in NYC. It was real, raw, and it involved an intimate exchange with another.

When it came to one of my birthdays on Maui, one of my friends went to the other side of the island to get some red clay to paint me. It never happened, a huge rainstorm, but I appreciate her gesture. However, the imprint is in me because out of my paintbrush came lots of images of Omos, with added embellishments from Michael's art store.

Invitation: Create what you want and what wants to come through you. I like having the Omos in my house. Whose life is it anyways?

My Healing Image

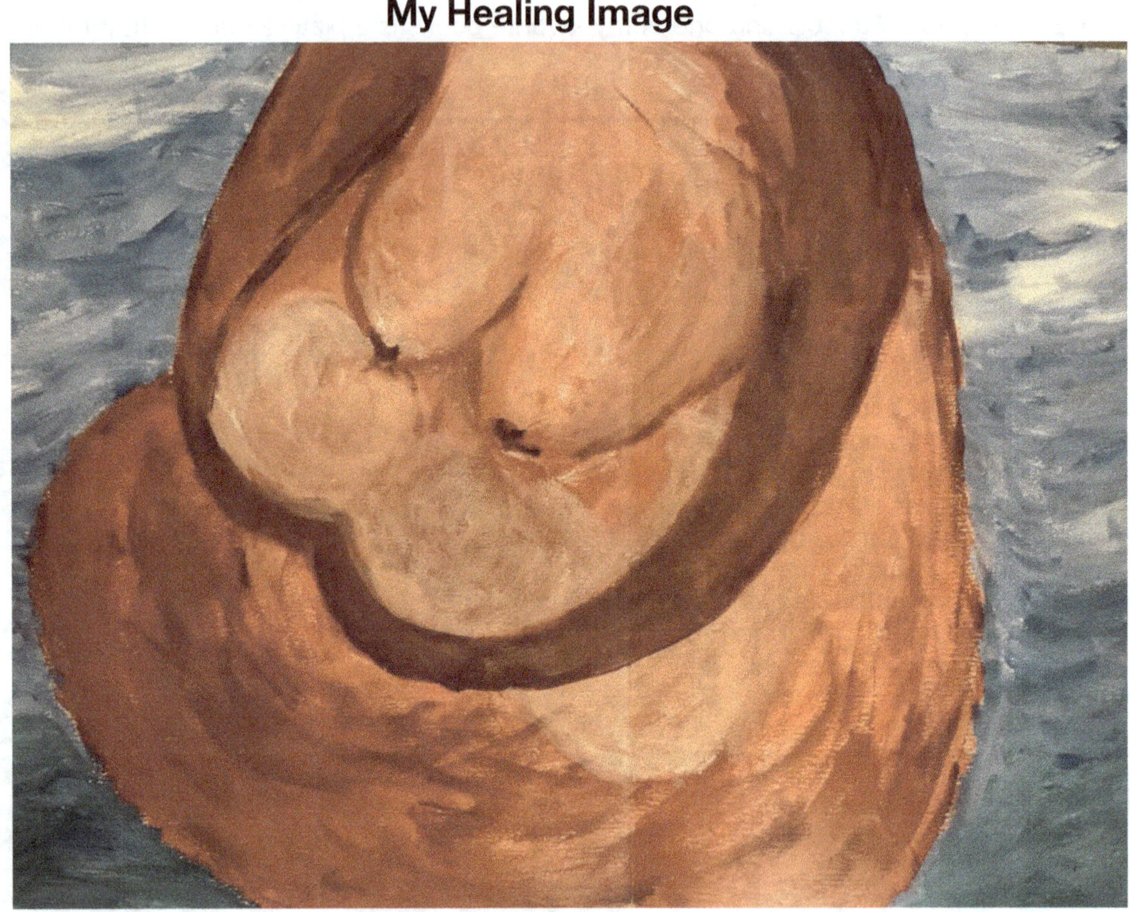

Birthing Workshop

Back in the early '90s there were two Spiritual Centers, one on the East Coast, Omega, and one on the West Coast, Esalen. Then one opened in the middle of the country, in Chicago. It was called Oasis Center for Human Potential, Oasis for short on Sheridan Road. It was in the old house I used to go to belonging to the Crown family, who were friends of my family. Doc Crown, as he was called, and his wife Becky, lived in that house and when they passed, their house became Oasis.

As a child I used to sit in their living room, quiet and behaving, while the adults talked and argued over who knows what. I grew up in an adult's world.

So, when I was called to do workshops there because the space was bigger than my Centers, it was an eerie feeling walking into rooms that were once filled with velvet furniture and staff. Now, the space was open with big pillows strewn on the floor, and the coffee machine in a room I wasn't allowed to go into in the past. Doc Crown was the doctor that assisted mother in my birth. This space was where I created 'Birthing Workshops.'

In the workshop, the drum took us out of time and space into the imprint of our births. Pictures were made and then hung on the walls. Looking at them, I felt as though I were in a hospital nursery, witnessing all their births.

Stories from deep in their imaginations poured out along with feelings that emerged that were hidden in the body.

From doing Birthing Workshops, I became aware that I was born into an environment of disappointment and abandonment. Mother, an only child, did not like to be alone. She wouldn't stay in the apartment alone, always going to her mother's house. I was told many people came to my birth, and then they left her alone to go out to celebrate, so the abandonment must have kicked in. Also, me being a first born, my family tradition wanted a boy first. By exploring through art, I became aware of why mother would say to me at random, "You're a big disappointment to me Sher, a big disappointment." It didn't hurt less, but it gave me a bit of understanding of its source.

I could never track the cause and effect about so much of what I was born into, and when I did, I offered the Birthing Workshop experience to the greater community.

Invitation: If you feel called, imagine your birth, the feelings, the themes, and draw it. There's something about taking an image out from inside, and bringing it out in the light of day.

Creating a Personal Altar

What is an Altar? My definition of an Altar is Your Sacred Space that when you see it, it transports you into another dimension of life. It is a reminder of the eternal, of the sacred, of other dimensions, of life and of ourselves.

Creating Your Altar opens your space to a dimension of spirituality and to what is Sacred to you. It can include:

- Sacred Deities
- Spiritual Teachers
- Photos
- Your Journal
- Flowers
- A Candle
- Natural Objects
- Tarot Cards
- Bells
- Stones
- Anything else that is Sacred to you

It can be an outdoor Altar, or one on your own desk. It opens your space to living at a multidimensional level.

My First Outdoor Altar

Gray/Green Beings

I may lose you on this one. I was living on Maui alone and some unusual things were happening for about a week before 'The Event' happened. I didn't put 2 & 2 together until afterwards, to see something was stirring.

The doorbell rang in the middle of the night, and when I went to answer, I opened the door, no one was there. Then I looked around and there was no doorbell. I'll spare you the other odd happenings. Then (take a breath) I was awakened in the middle of the night and I saw, standing next to my bed, four gray/green Beings with huge eyes. And, I was paralyzed, couldn't move, couldn't speak.

Sleeping naked with only a sheet, no AC, I managed to make sounds though my jaw was clamped shut. "What do you want?" I mumbled, barely audible to myself. I tried to move but I was paralyzed. Time stood still and the next thing I remember, it was morning.

I never mentioned this to anyone for years, until I was living in Ashland, OR. My boyfriend would go to the metaphysical library in town to rent videos on UFOs and watch one each night. I wasn't into it, but one night he asked if I would watch one with him. So we were watching one where people all over the globe were being interviewed. Each one said the very same thing, "There were four of them, green or gray beings with big eyes and I felt paralyzed." I gasped, it came back and I said, "That happened to me when I was living on Maui!" I hadn't doubted that it was real back then, but I haven't been one to share my Sacred Spiritual experiences. They are personal.

I'm including this because I feel a connection to the Galactic Universe in ways that are familiar to my Soul. Also, have you experienced any other-worldly experiences?

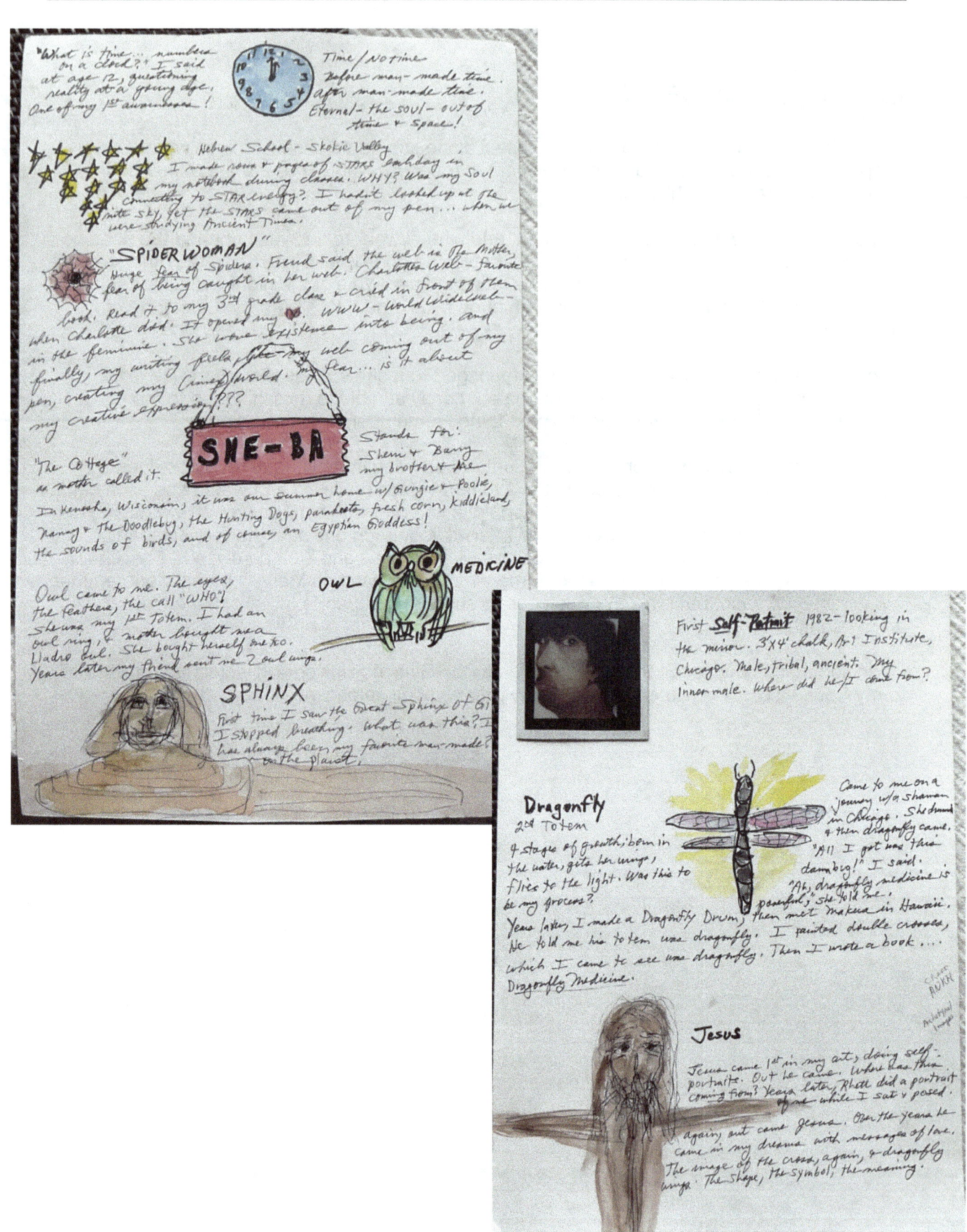

"What is time... numbers on a cloud?" I said at age 12, questioning reality at a young age. One of my 1st awarenesses!

Time / No Time
before man-made time. after man-made time. Eternal - the SOUL - out of time & space!

Hebrew School - Skokie Valley
I made rows & pages of STARS each day in my notebook during classes. WHY? Was my soul connecting to STAR energy? I hadn't looked up at the nite sky, yet the STARS came out of my pen... when we were studying Ancient Times.

"SPIDER WOMAN"
Huge fear of Spiders. Freud said the web is the Mother. Charlotte's Web - favorite fear of being caught in her web. book. Read it to my 3rd grade class & cried in front of them when Charlotte died. It opened my ♥. WWW - World Wide Web - in the feminine. She wove existence into being. and finally, my writing feels like my web coming out of my pen, creating my (inner) world. my fear... is it about my creative expression???

SHE-BA
Stands for: Sheri & Barry my brother & me
"The Cottage" as mother called it.
In Kenosha, Wisconsin, it was our summer home w/ Gungie & Poolie, Nancy & the Doodlebug, the Hunting Dogs, parakeets, fresh corn, kiddieland, the sounds of birds, and of course, an Egyptian Goddess!

OWL MEDICINE
Owl came to me. The eyes, the feathers, the call "WHO"? She was my 1st Totem. I had an owl ring, & mother bought me a Lladro owl. She bought herself one too. Years later my friend sent me 2 owl wings.

SPHINX
First time I saw the Great Sphinx of Giza I stopped breathing. What was this? It has always been my favorite man-made? in the past.

First Self-Portrait 1982 - looking in the mirror. 3'x4' chalk, Art Institute, Chicago. Male, tribal, ancient. My inner male. Where did he/I come from?

Dragonfly
2nd Totem
4 stages of growth; born in the water, gets her wings, flies to the light. Was this to be my process?
Years later, I made a Dragonfly Drum, then met Makua in Hawaii. He told me his totem was dragonfly. I painted double crosses, which I came to see was dragonfly. Then I wrote a book.... Dragonfly Medicine.

Came to me on a journey w/ a shaman in Chicago. She drummed & then dragonfly came. "All I got was this damn bug!" I said. "Ah, dragonfly medicine is powerful," she told me.

Jesus
Jesus came 1st in my art, doing self-portraits. Out he came. Where was this coming from? Years later, Rhett did a portrait of me while I sat & posed. again, out came Jesus. Over the years he came in my dreams with messages of love. The image of the cross, again, & dragonfly wings. The shape, the symbol, the meaning.

Symbols - A Visual Life Review

Invitation: Create a visual diary using symbols that have meaning for your life review. This is a part of my version.

Sherri Shulman, M.A.A.T., ATR, Founder and Director of the **Center For Creative Psychotherapy, Ltd.** is a registered Art Therapist, group leader, teacher and lecturer who brings to the field a creative approach toward individual growth, development, and healing.

Sherri earned her Masters of Art in Art Therapy at the Art Institute of Chicago in affiliation with Rush Presbetarian St. Lukes Psychiatry Department. She is a member of the Illinois Art Therapy Association and the American Art Therapy Association.

Sherri has been on staff at Illinois Masonic Hospital, has appeared on Chicago's own **Two On 2**, and has been interviewed in numerous publications including a feature article in **Today's Chicago Woman.** Having coined the term Creative Psychotherapy, Sherri uses this holistic approach facilitating personal growth and development with both individuals and groups. As a leader in her field Sherri has taken her application of Art/Psychotherapy out of the traditional setting of hospitals and psychiatric environments into the general public with individuals who are already functioning at a very high level and are seeking further self understanding.

Center for Creative Psychotherapy

Back in Chicago from the mid '80s to almost the mid '90s I opened three Centers. There were five ongoing groups. Each group met weekly and lasted for five years each.

Every week I brought ideas and topics for them to create from, invitations for exploring feelings. Mostly, they used colored chalks and 18" x 24" paper.

When I think back to those experiences my heart swells with joy. The level of their commitment and mine to growth, friendships, exploring in a new field, allowing feelings and themes to emerge...I am so touched. To be able to Journey so closely with groups and individuals and for that length of time...the memories are irreplaceable.

It seems dream-like, in the now, where we push buttons for instant connection, but back then it was a haven, a place on the planet that seems magical in memory. They knew me as Sherri Shulman. My name as well as myself has gone through many evolutions since then.

"To all who walked through those Sacred Doorways with me, I am crying tears of gratitude for the Journey we navigated together. Blessings on your Journey." Love, Sherri

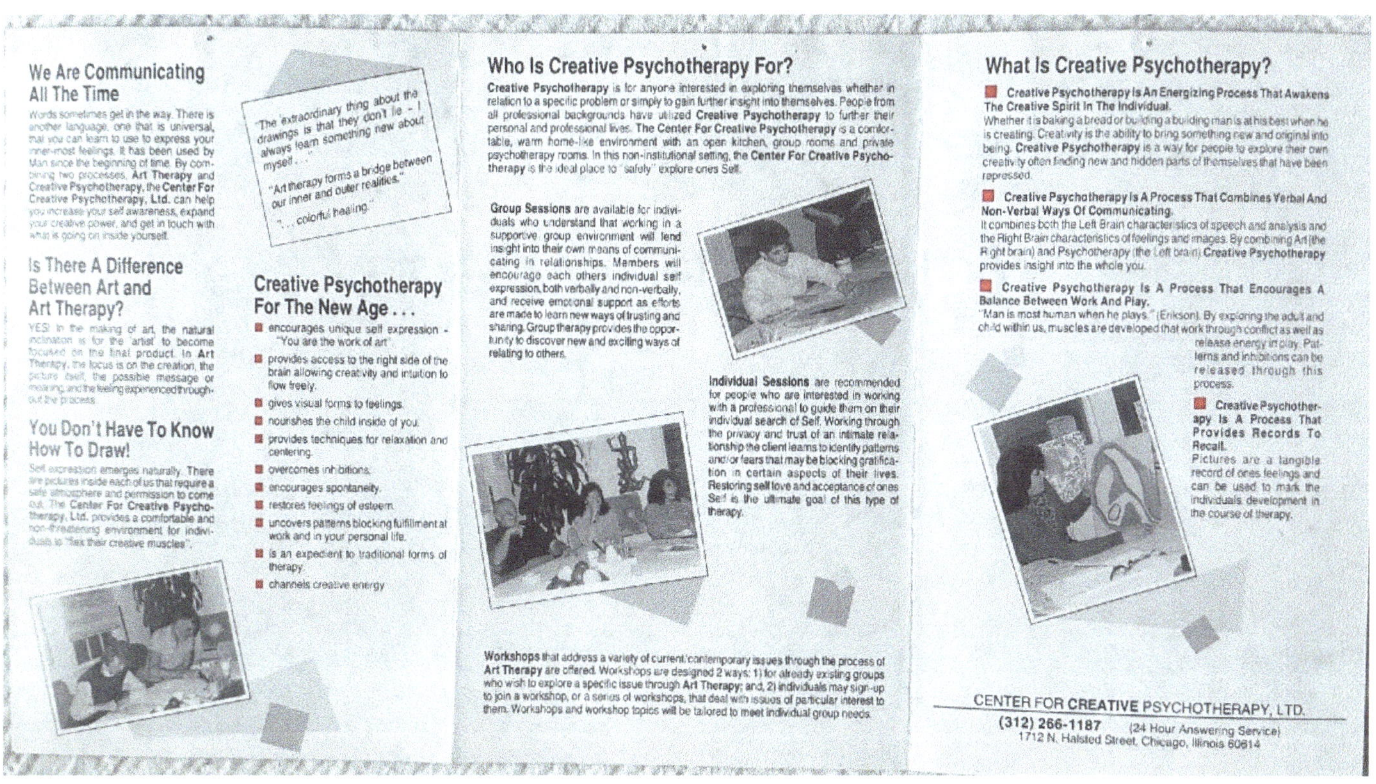

We Are Communicating All The Time

Words sometimes get in the way. There is another language, one that is universal, that you can learn to use to express your inner-most feelings. It has been used by Man since the beginning of time. By combining two processes, Art Therapy and Creative Psychotherapy, the Center For Creative Psychotherapy, Ltd. can help you increase your self awareness, expand your creative power, and get in touch with what is going on inside yourself.

Is There A Difference Between Art and Art Therapy?

YES! In the making of art, the natural inclination is for the 'artist' to become focused on the final product. In Art Therapy, the focus is on the creation, the picture itself, the possible message or meaning, and the feeling experienced throughout the process.

You Don't Have To Know How To Draw!

Self expression emerges naturally. There are pictures inside each of us that require a safe atmosphere and permission to come out. The Center For Creative Psychotherapy, Ltd. provides a comfortable and non-threatening environment for individuals to "flex their creative muscles".

"The extraordinary thing about the drawings is that they don't lie – I always learn something new about myself . . ."

"Art therapy forms a bridge between our inner and outer realities."

". . . colorful healing"

Creative Psychotherapy For The New Age . . .

- encourages unique self expression - "You are the work of art".
- provides access to the right side of the brain allowing creativity and intuition to flow freely.
- gives visual forms to feelings.
- nourishes the child inside of you.
- provides techniques for relaxation and centering.
- overcomes inhibitions.
- encourages spontaneity.
- restores feelings of esteem.
- uncovers patterns blocking fulfillment at work and in your personal life.
- is an expedient to traditional forms of therapy.
- channels creative energy

Who Is Creative Psychotherapy For?

Creative Psychotherapy is for anyone interested in exploring themselves whether in relation to a specific problem or simply to gain further insight into themselves. People from all professional backgrounds have utilized Creative Psychotherapy to further their personal and professional lives. The Center For Creative Psychotherapy is a comfortable, warm home-like environment with an open kitchen, group rooms and private psychotherapy rooms. In this non-institutional setting, the Center For Creative Psychotherapy is the ideal place to "safely" explore ones Self.

Group Sessions are available for individuals who understand that working in a supportive group environment will lend insight into their own means of communicating in relationships. Members will encourage each others individual self expression, both verbally and non-verbally, and receive emotional support as efforts are made to learn new ways of trusting and sharing. Group therapy provides the opportunity to discover new and exciting ways of relating to others.

Individual Sessions are recommended for people who are interested in working with a professional to guide them on their individual search of Self. Working through the privacy and trust of an intimate relationship the client learns to identify patterns and/or fears that may be blocking gratification in certain aspects of their lives. Restoring self love and acceptance of ones Self is the ultimate goal of this type of therapy.

Workshops that address a variety of current/contemporary issues through the process of Art Therapy are offered. Workshops are designed 2 ways: 1) for already existing groups who wish to explore a specific issue through Art Therapy; and, 2) individuals may sign-up to join a workshop, or a series of workshops, that deal with issues of particular interest to them. Workshops and workshop topics will be tailored to meet individual group needs.

What Is Creative Psychotherapy?

Creative Psychotherapy Is An Energizing Process That Awakens The Creative Spirit In The Individual.
Whether it is baking a bread or building a building man is at his best when he is creating. Creativity is the ability to bring something new and original into being. Creative Psychotherapy is a way for people to explore their own creativity often finding new and hidden parts of themselves that have been repressed.

Creative Psychotherapy Is A Process That Combines Verbal And Non-Verbal Ways Of Communicating.
It combines both the Left Brain characteristics of speech and analysis and the Right Brain characteristics of feelings and images. By combining Art (the Right brain) and Psychotherapy (the Left brain) Creative Psychotherapy provides insight into the whole you.

Creative Psychotherapy Is A Process That Encourages A Balance Between Work And Play.
"Man is most human when he plays." (Erikson). By exploring the adult and child within us, muscles are developed that work through conflict as well as release energy in play. Patterns and inhibitions can be released through this process.

Creative Psychotherapy Is A Process That Provides Records To Recall.
Pictures are a tangible record of ones feelings and can be used to mark the individuals development in the course of therapy.

CENTER FOR **CREATIVE** PSYCHOTHERAPY, LTD.
(312) 266-1187   (24 Hour Answering Service)
1712 N. Halsted Street, Chicago, Illinois 60614

An Invitation to Make Music

Invitation: A Most Powerful Word

You may wonder why I include the word Invitation with my posts?

It began when I was studying to be an art therapist at the School of the Art Institute in Chicago. We were required to experience two field work placements. At that time, Art Therapy was not known in the larger community at all. It was the early '80s and it was used with Veterans and the elderly. I spoke to the head of the department and assured him that I would fulfill the requirements of those placements, however, I wanted to take Art Therapy into the larger community of high functioning people. So I asked him, "In addition to the two field work sites I am required to fulfill, I would like additional supervision for the two groups I will create because I will be opening a Center for the greater public to attend and I will pay for the auxiliary supervision."

He said quizzically, "Where are you going to get the people?" "Oh, I'll get the people." I said confidently, hiding the fear deep inside. "Can you provide the supervision?"

We agreed. I made a flyer that inspired something in the heart and soul of many of those who read it. In the course of the coming days, I met people, as we do, in coffee shops, at the museum, you know, out and about. If someone looked somewhat open, I introduced myself, met them in their frequency, showed them a flyer, and 'invited' them to be part of something new.

In a very short time, two groups of ten each were formed and I rented a space at night in a children's playhouse setting, and together we began a Journey.

The groups continued for years, and I believe it was the 'invitation' along with destiny, that transported Art Therapy out of the facilities and into the culture that was open to meet it. With an invitation, our inner child, inner self, inner critic, allows for choice. It has an opportunity to feel included, chosen, wanted, cared-about, which overrides the mind, and fear, and creates a freer space to consider something new.

Invitation: Try it out on yourself. Invite a part of Yourself to _____. Notice how that feels.

Nambé Tribe Candelabra

Rituals

Rituals are a part of our lives. All of us do them. The ones we're not happy about are called addictions. I would like to offer a personal relationship to 'Ritual' where we create unique, personal, and meaningful ones that support our lives in Sacred Ways.

My 'Candlelighting Ritual'

I have a candelabra made by the Nambe Tribe here in New Mexico. It's called "the Tree of Life." Any time I want to lite-up and call-in support from the bigger Light, I take to my candelabra, Tree of Life/Light for a special occasion such as a friend's birthday, or what I want to light up in my own Journey. It's a way of honoring and asking for support from the Light of the Universe. For friends' birthdays I like to take out my Tree of Light and create a ceremony where the person lites-up whatever areas of their life they are ready to embody, and they speak into it aloud. If others are present, they may participate by lighting a candle with a wish for their friend.

SACRED RITUAL

In Israel, in 1990, with a group of 500, we journeyed to the sacred site of a mountain called Masada, where, in Ancient times, 960 Jewish men, women and children committed a mass suicide rather than surrender to being captured, tortured, and murdered by the army below. A somber experience turned into a Sacred Ritual/Ceremony as we were given lit candles to carry and walk with down the mountain at sunset. I was one of the first in the procession so I got to the bottom and looked up to see hundreds of lights meandering down the mountainside. It was an out of time ritual that is alive to me as I write this to You.

Life itself, can carry many rituals depending on how we meet a moment, a memory or celebration.

Flipping the switch into the Sacred Dimension is the key that makes a ritual come alive.

Invitation: Honor yourself and Your own Customized Ritual Space.

Angels

The appearance of Angels can come in many forms. Back in the '80s in Chicago, I was working as a docent at the Museum of Contemporary Art, giving tours to adults and children's school groups. My tours were colorful and filled with questions, possibilities, and invitations. After one tour, someone came up to me and said something very unusual, "You should go to Santa Fe." I don't know why she said this to me, but a week later I was in Santa Fe. I took her advice and didn't want to waste a moment.

When I arrived, I went to a coffee shop and saw people in ripped jeans (before our time now) and hair uncombed and wild and all I could say and kept saying was, "You can live like this?" I was living in high-rises in fancy Chicago, yet my Soul was magnetized to, and yearning for, this different Way of Life. This Angel delivered the Customized Message to me. Of course, it would take years for me to change my life and move there, but the imprint was made. (I've always said, "I just need the imprint.")

Another Angel crossed paths with me at the Museum of Contemporary Art on one of my tours. She approached me after a tour, and said, "You should be an Art Therapist." Art and Therapy, the two areas that were close in my heart. I couldn't believe there was such a field as Art Therapy. The next day I called and made an interview with the head of the Art Therapy department of the School of the Art Institute in Chicago. I was accepted into the program, but first I had to take some courses and create a portfolio to qualify, which I did.

Angels can come in different forms. People can be angels and deliver messages that are life changing and Custom for your Journey.

Then there are angels without form that can come in the Dream Time, or in Journey Space, or in any altered state, and in Your Art. They are messengers.

Being Initiated by the Angels

My Process

The Birthing of Dancing Snake Woman and her sister Sky Snake Woman

Many years ago, while walking on what I call 'the Camino' (my Custom version in Santa Fe), I saw and picked up a stick that formed into a long V at the top. It looked like a Divining Rod and felt sturdy and balanced in my hand. The stick sat in my basket of favorite poles and sticks until just the right moment came for it to inspire the next leg of her Journey.

Moving around with my stick in hand, shaking it, getting a feel for it, we both knew her time had come to evolve, as did mine. So I gathered lots of materials on my 60" round art table. Feathers, furs, cowry shells, glue gun, African Mud Cloth. They were all getting ready to COOK, coming alive. There's a magic in the air for me when I sense a transformation is about to take place. My blood flows faster, my heart races and I begin to move into an Altered State. Something is about to be born, and I have no clue how it/she will look, feel, and become a presence in my world, both outer and inner.

In this Altered State, I huff and puff, breathing heavily and surrender to what wants to be born. That's why my creations feel alive to me. My favorite quality in life is aliveness itself. My stick came alive and became Dancing Snake Woman. She became two snakes, her bottom half became Dancing Snake Woman, and her upper branches became her sister, Sky Snake Woman. She carries a presence, and a rattle goes with her.

Timing is important in our Creative Process. There's a moment when the inner meets the outer. Overriding is not necessary, listening on the inner and being sensitive to that moment, Your Moment, is a way we fine-tune our relationship to the presence that is wanting to be seen.

Dancing Snake Woman & Her Sister, Sky Snake Woman

Names

What's in a name? A lot.

Being in the right Name has been important to me. I can't tell you how many women have shared with me they don't like their name.

After I got divorced, I kept my husband's name for a while because it was my professional name, but that didn't last long.

In many tribal cultures, people are called to change their name according to personal initiations and rites of passage. That has happened for me in my life. As I have navigated different chapters and Sacred Moments in my life, names appeared in ways that were Customized for me, and I embraced them, though I have kept many of the initiations and names that were given as private and personal.

Each name was an invitation to claim another aspect of my Soul's Journey. Each name represented a chapter of my life. I take these messages that were delivered to me personally as Sacred Names that carried an invitation. Whether one chooses to formalize it for the record, have their friends call them a different name, or secretly bond with what you know your Soul to be speaking personally to you, the choice is Yours. Even my house has a name...Casa Svetlana, which means House of Light.

Invitation: Tune into, notice, welcome, invite, seen and unseen aspects of your Self to be revealed.

Svetlana Means Light in Russian

**My Girls (the Hens) &
Blanco (the Rooster)**

Wolf Medicine

Animal Medicine

Animal Totem Pole in the Chakras

Back in the day, I did a couple of groups I called Animal Totem Pole, where I drummed for each of the chakras to see what animals would appear for them. They would be the guardians of that chakra.

Animal medicine is close in my heart. I have done dozens of pictures and series of animals: Lions, Elephants, Horses, Wolves, Chickens, Roosters, so many! Different animals appear at certain times on our Journey with Custom messages. However, this experience is an invitation that invites the animal kingdom to come forward deliberately as a group. It's an established community of support for the long haul.

I recommend the book Animal-Speak by Ted Andrews (you probably have it already)
Invitation: Find some drum music on the internet and go into a semi-altered state. One by one, open each chakra and invite an animal to appear. Thank them when they do (they like that.) Then draw your customized Totem Pole. It's an out-picturing of who has shown up for you, offering their guidance in a Sacred Way.

My Tribute to Cecil after a poacher murdered him

My Indoor Art Studio

Studios...Indoor and Out

Anything can be a studio: a small bedroom, part of a garage, a table, your car, your art bag. It's about giving a space an 'identity.'

In the realm of Creativity, we are not put here to watch other people's version. That's fine, but that's not all there is. Once I wondered what it would be like to write a song, and asked myself, how does someone do that? So I gave it a go and wrote one. Not too good. Belongs in the "Michael Row Your Boat Ashore" category, but I tried it. High five!

WE DON'T HAVE TO QUALIFY TO BE A CREATIVE!

It's an imprint in our Soul.

WE are the studio. You can create a beautiful and elaborate studio, and never use it. You can wish for the space to have a studio in. You can create the studio of your dreams, and I have, both indoor and outdoor, and still you may not be in the FLOW.

Flow happens when it happens. It's an 'inside job.' Not to say, it isn't fun to have a studio, but don't confuse it from the actual creative process that comes from the bigger, immeasurable studio, our SOUL.

The Ancient Egyptians had their version of attempting to measure the Soul after death through "The Weighing of the Heart" Ceremony. In my world, they weren't even close. We get to explore our own relationship to Soul, one realm of which I am calling Our Creative Soul.

Invitation- Claim: "I am my Studio. I have access to FLOW. I am a Creative Soul!"

Going Public

Art Therapy Openings

We had openings, like an art gallery would. I know it may seem normal and ordinary now, but back in the '80s, therapy was hidden, with a capital H. Not in my world!

At our first opening, someone from a news program from TV must have been there, because I received a phone call, asking if a crew could film a group of Art Therapy in process and interview some clients as well as me.

I asked for volunteers. It was scary, I was scared, but we did it and appeared on "Two on Two." Well, one thing led to another and I had more openings at my Centers. Then, we went even more public and had an opening in a restaurant.

Of course, there were Christmas parties too, where someone played the guitar, there was catering, we sang, we mingled. We reclaimed parts of ourselves. We created community.

Invitation:

1) Start showing your creative work to another. Take a stand for your creative Truth and your Creative Soul. It's about sharing, not evaluating. This is a Sacred Gift to your Soul. Let the 'other' know it's coming from inner work and not to be looked at solely as a work of art. It's Your Creative Soul, and it has meaning.

2) Make a Creative Date with someone. Remember, You are the ultimate Work of Art. Dust off your courage and stand for that!

Customize Your Creative Life

Please keep an open mind on this one. Have there been experiences you wanted to try but the form or timing of them stood in the way? For example, maybe you wanted to try something out but the commitment of 10 sessions was too much of an investment, or the time was not fitting into your life.

Well, I can relate. I have taken many classes that were 'private sessions' back in the day, when I didn't have the time to do them in the forms they were offered. By approaching the instructor and asking if I could take the workshop privately, we were able to work out an arrangement that fit for both of us. All was agreed upon up front.

I made baskets, did stained-glass, took public speaking (had fun but it didn't override my fears), made a book out of paper with rose petals I brought in. My life was so full I literally did not have the time.

The reason I'm sharing this is, if there is something you have the desire to learn, explore, or express, and it doesn't fit your circumstances or attention span, you can inquire. It's part of my version on 'Customizing.'

Sometimes it's a fit, other times not so much. We're just seeing if there's space for what will fit into your needs and interests.

Invitation: Customize Your Creative Life!

P.S. Customize Your Creative Life
(whatever that means for you)

I love lotuses and I created my first Stained Glass Lotus design with a Crystal in her center

Sacred Memories

There are Moments...which are sacred Treasures on your Journey.
Invitation: Create a 'Sacred Memory Box' and/or cover a sketchbook with fabric, or buy something fab you're drawn to.

There are pictures, images, moments, memories, stories that are Sacred, Special to You, touching you at the heart and soul level. The invitation is to record them in a special Way. Write down a headline, a few words, a sketch, a snapshot of a moment or a feeling that touched you, that was Sacred to you. Use scratch paper, it can be in the form of an original deck of cards, kept in Your Sacred Memory Box.

Some of mine are:
- A giraffe licking food from my hand
- African women bending over in a line on a golf course, tearing the grass with their hands on a green, and placing it on a blanket that they kept moving
- Elephants in chains being walked down the large paths at 6:00 AM, before Lincoln Park Zoo opened to the public
- A "kill" of a lion killing a zebra right next to our Rover that got stuck in the mud, no roads, no elaborate communication system, walkie-talkie till we were rescued with a rope thrown to pull us out
- Riding donkeys on the island of Santorini with my father following behind me on his donkey

That's all I can write for publication (if you know what I mean)

Painting Pictures With Words

I love words. The right word opens doorways for me. Some of my clients took to writing down the words and phrases I used in my sessions. One woman named them, "Shoshanaisms." I'm offering some of them for you to be inspired to create your own. It's part of my style, and they are fun, creative, colorful, and sometimes memorable. You may recognize some of these.

-I don't sit on a rickety chair because I know I'm going down
-Being interruptible
-Can't beat someone at Their Game
-The One Wrong Move Syndrome
-Making Peace with the Flow
-The Truth is the Prettiest Picture
-Stuck on Send
-All Petals Open
-Looking for Goldilocks (finding the middle)
-Pebble in the Shoe
-The end doesn't justify the means
-Born with a Job
-Being in the Driver's Seat of Your Life
-Roles not Relationships
-Talking Story (we say this in Hawaii)
-Being in the Right Question
-Reporting versus Sharing
-Moving the Whole Self Forward
-It's a God-Job
-Watered-down Version
-At the Level
-Things are right where we left them

Healing with Words & Sound

Some of us had the experience of hearing words and labels that were cruel. We call it residue, or trauma. And often, it's not just the words but the emotion that delivered them. Words hurt and words can heal if the energy of Heart can deliver them. They have left imprints in our "Emotional Soul" and some of them have been carried over many generations and lifetimes.

Invitation: Write down in your handwriting, the words and phrases that hurt you. Take a breath and feel the love you have for yourself, and then, write and read aloud, your response that overrides those words and fill it with love so that your inner child self will trust the love you are offering. Deeply open to receive the new imprint, and then relax and surrender to feeling the love that You are.

Shutters (My first picture ever, age 21)

Boy in the Doorway (2nd Picture)

Healing with Art: The Healing Image

Creativity is the doorway to our emotional soul. Our images can stir feelings that we didn't have words for. Doing a "feelings picture" is a great warm up and triggers the Emotional Soul and the Creative Soul to connect.

In my first ever picture in art school, Shutters, the drapes were closed, and in the second picture, Boy in the Doorway, the boy was barely opening the door.

When Art Therapy came into my world, I opened the drapes, and walked through the doorway. One brush stroke can open a Path of exploring your Creative Truths.

An image came in a dream years ago, and I didn't know what it meant at the time. It was a Golden Eagle that flew right up to my face. We were face to face with each other. Now I know it's meaning. The messages in our art may not be revealed at the moment that the image comes through. This picture, which has always been special and Sacred to me, finally delivered its message. "We are ONE." And I pass that to You.

I finally found my Community…

WE ARE THE CREATIVES!

Golden Eagle & Me

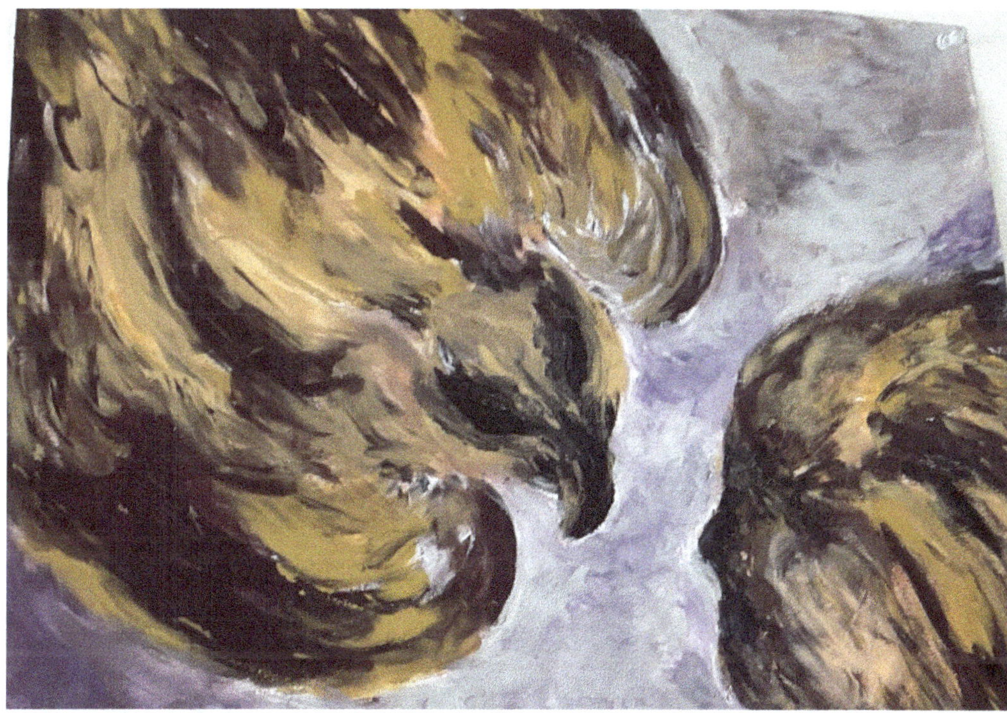

In Gratitude…

To the Friends who Journeyed with me on Facebook... YOU brought the Faces to my Book.
It meant the world to me when I'd see your names...and I would conjure up your faces and I felt
your hearts. All that love and support filled in the holes and deep grooves of its absence. I felt
cared about, seen, heard, and met. Your gift has helped me to heal and to feel part of a
community.

WE ARE THE CREATIVES, unique, unusual, original, who customize our relationship to life.
There are so many groups that people identify with: The Yoga Path, The Tantra Path, Dancing,
Environmental, Bikers, Animals and on and on. Your response and support brought the group
feeling together and we became a community I call "The Creatives," our original, unusual
relationship to life.

When I decided to write this book, I chose to write what I hoped would be an offering, a
contribution to our self-expression and our Creative Soul, especially in a time of such
destruction. Michelle Obama offered us "When they go low, we go high." My version is, "When
faced with destruction, we turn to Creation."

You will always be in my heart. I felt your presence every step through my Journey, and it felt
wonderful. May you feel the joy, the satisfaction, the wonder, and the deep gratitude of being
the ones on the planet who have come to explore and know YOUR CREATIVE SOUL.

On this Sacred Journey of life, in this time space reality, you have blessed my life and my Soul.
To walk so intimately with a part of your Soul meeting mine, these footprints I treasure. You are
original, you are perfection, no mistakes, no finishing touches. As is...you are the Ultimate work
of Art.

Till we meet again...thank you for Journeying with me.   Eternal Gratitude.

And to Elli...

And to Elli, who Journeyed with me, so closely, meeting my needs every step of the Way, bringing fun, laughter, understanding, and levels and capabilities that supported my Journey in ways that are truly a God-Job.

Every step was fun together. It felt like we danced our way through this Journey.
Elli, you were my perfect midwife, who came to support me in every way...you touched places in me that your love healed. I will always remember your gifts of sisterhood and your Creative Soul.

I am eternally grateful to have Journeyed together in such Sacred Ways, and for all of your sacred gifts and the intimacy we shared.
Heart to heart, dear soul sister. You are eternally in mine.

Elli and Me

The Joy of Communing with Sisters Across the Ocean

Habitat as a Work of Art

Garden of Eden

Bird Sanctuary